ROSE SCENTED MURDER

ALSO BY JILL PATERSON

The Celtic Dagger

Murder At The Rocks

Once Upon A Lie

Lane's End

Deadly Investment

Poisoned Palette

The Fourth String

ROSE SCENTED MURDER

A FITZJOHN MYSTERY

JILL PATERSON

ISBN 978-0-9925840-7-8

Publisher: J. Henderson, Australia

Publication Date: March 29th, 2019

A catalogue record for this
book is available from the
National Library of Australia

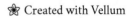

❀ Created with Vellum

For Valerie and Anne

CHAPTER 1

*I*rritated, Dolores slammed the door to the costume department and, in an atmosphere charged with the expectation of the imminent matinee performance, shoved her way against the surge of cast members and headed towards Howard Greenwood's dressing room. Clutching the only remaining costume that she believed would fit Howard's expanding girth, she felt herself jostled with each step as her anger towards him intensified. Her heart quickened when she reached his door and found it ajar. Pausing in an effort to regain her composure, she called out above the din, 'Howard, it's Dolores. I have that substitute costume for you to try on.' When no reply came she threw the door open. 'Look mister high and mighty, I don't know who you think you are but... *good god! Someone, help!*' she screamed at the sight of Howard's body splayed in the centre of the room, his once blue eyes now clouded and staring.

'Call an ambulance,' rang out a voice from those now crammed in the doorway.

Dolores turned to the sea of gaping faces. 'It's too late. He's dead.'

CHAPTER 2

*F*itzjohn dusted his hands off against his old faded beige trousers and closed the greenhouse door with a sense of satisfaction after tending his orchids. Breathing in the fresh overcast morning air, he walked leisurely back through the garden towards the house, observing the new seedlings in each flower bed as he went. He hesitated when he reached the jacaranda tree and pushing his wire-framed glasses up along the bridge of his nose, looked up into its branches where a flock of rainbow lorikeets sat chirping their dissatisfaction at his tardiness in filling the birdfeeder. With a chuckle, he did so amongst the flurry of flapping wings before making his way into the house to prepare to leave for the police station.

Half an hour later, he descended the stairs dressed in a dark grey suit and maroon tie which he adjusted in the hall mirror before smoothing down the few remaining wisps of hair on top of his head. As he did so, the doorbell sounded and on opening the door, he found his young sergeant, Martin Betts. 'Betts. I wasn't expecting you to pick me up this morning. I've ordered a cab.'

'I was passing on my way to the station, sir, and thought you might like a lift instead.'

'Passing? But I thought you'd already moved into your new apartment on the other side of the harbour,' replied Fitzjohn somewhat perplexed.

'I have, sir,' Betts replied, craning his neck past Fitzjohn toward the kitchen doorway at the end of the hall.

'In that case, it's been rather a circuitous route for you, hasn't it? Can I get you something? A cup of coffee perhaps?'

'No, I'm fine, sir.'

'Are you sure? You seem a bit on edge,' continued Fitzjohn, giving Betts a quizzical look.

'I'm sure, sir. Really.'

'Very well,' replied Fitzjohn still not convinced. 'I'll just cancel my cab and then we can be on our way.' As Fitzjohn did so, Betts peered up the stairwell before his gaze went through the archway into the living room. 'You're not fine, are you?' said Fitzjohn, slipping his phone back into his pocket and grabbing his briefcase from the hall table. 'Something's bothering you?'

'No, sir.'

'Well, that being so, my next question is, are you on some kind of fact finding mission?' Betts' face paled. 'You are, aren't you?'

'I don't know what you mean, sir.'

'Come on, Betts. You must think I came down in the last shower of rain,' replied Fitzjohn as he studied his young sergeant's face. 'What is it, another bet cooked up by our esteemed duty officer?' Betts' face reddened. 'What sort of wager is it this time? No, let me guess. You've been sent to find out whether or not you'd find Chief Superintendent Ashby here, haven't you?' Betts swallowed hard. 'I thought as much. Well, as you can see, she isn't here.' Fitzjohn turned and opened the front door. 'How much did you lose? On second thought, don't answer that. I don't want to know,' he added as he stepped outside.

'How did you know, sir,' asked Betts as Fitzjohn locked the door behind them.

'I'm a detective,' Fitzjohn replied as he climbed into the car.

For the first five minutes of their journey into town, the two officers travelled in silence before Betts asked, 'Would you like to drop in at the Charlotte Café, sir. I'll buy you breakfast. As a peace offering.'

'Don't grovel Betts. It doesn't become you.' As Fitzjohn spoke his mobile phone rang. 'Fitzjohn. Yes, ma'am. I see. Very well, we're on our way.' Fitzjohn slipped his phone back into his pocket and turned to Betts. 'We've been asked to attend a homicide in the city at the Adelphi Theatre. An actor by the name of Howard Greenwood was found dead in his dressing room this morning.'

CHAPTER 3

When the theatre came into view, Fitzjohn peered out of the passenger car window with a sense of disappointment. In the broad light of day, the building's dilapidated façade imparted an atmosphere of desertion with its damaged signage board groaning with the force of the wind and its windows opaque and dirty. Not only did the building give testimony to a bygone era but justification for its imminent closure according to the notice pasted on the glass front door.

'I remember bringing Edith here to see a play some years ago,' Fitzjohn mused as the two officers climbed out of the car. 'She was very taken with the opulent interior as I remember. I think it gave her as much pleasure as the play itself with walls of silk wallpaper, gilded plasterwork, and chandeliers. I'm sure it would sadden her to see its crumbling state now.'

'Hopefully the inside has withstood the test of time a little better than the outside, sir,' said Betts as he led the way past a row of police cars in the lane that ran along the side of the building. Met by a constable on duty at the stage door, they showed their warrant cards and stepped inside to be met with a musty odour of stale recycled air and greeted by yet another police officer. 'I'm DCI Fitzjohn and this is DS Betts,' said Fitzjohn as his eyes travelled the length of the long narrow passageway before them. 'Where can we find the victim?'

'In his dressing room, sir. Turn right at the end of this passageway. It's half way down. The forensic pathologist and a team of scene of crime officers have already arrived and are with him now.'

'Anything else we should know?' asked Fitzjohn.

'Yes, sir. The people who were in the building at the time the body was discovered have been asked to wait in the auditorium.'

'Very good, Sergeant. Perhaps you can assist DS Betts in taking statements.'

As Betts and the sergeant left, Fitzjohn continued on along the dimly lit passage, taking in each dressing room as he went until, after turning right, his way became blocked by police tape. Ducking underneath, he stood on the threshold of a small room cluttered with odd bits of furniture, and clothing hung on a metal rack. A dresser, its surface covered with jars and containers, presumably of stage makeup, sat before a large mirror, its edge encircled with lights. Amid this disarray, two scene of crime officers went about their work while the pathologist, Charles Conroy, could be seen kneeling beside the victim's body. Wearing a single-breasted tail coat and white tie, his facial features and lifeless eyes accentuated with makeup, Howard Greenwood lay on his back, his torso covered with long-stemmed red roses. Cautiously, as he walked into the room, Fitzjohn stepped over an upturned crystal vase resting on the floor nearby along with a top hat and silver handled cane.

'Morning Charles.'

'Ah, Alistair, good morning. How've you been keeping?'

'Not too bad and yourself?' asked Fitzjohn.

'I can't complain.'

'I wonder if the roses have any significance,' said Fitzjohn looking down at the victim.

'A bit of theatrics, I suspect. Nothing more,' replied Charles. 'After all, it suits the environment, don't you think?' he added, looking around.

Fitzjohn followed his gaze to the myriad of champagne flutes and empty bottles that littered the room. 'It certainly looks like there was some sort of festivity in here last night.'

'It does,' replied Charles. 'The question is, who left last?'

'The killer might not have attended the celebration,' said Fitzjohn.

'Ah, good point. I hadn't thought of that,' said Charles. 'It must be the reason why you're the detective and I'm the pathologist,' he added with a chuckle as one of the SOCOs knelt down to remove each rose from the body.

'Have you any idea how he died?' asked Fitzjohn.

'He suffered a blow to the left temple, here,' replied Charles, pointing to the bruised area. 'The question is, was it the cause of death? The reason I say that is because he looks to be in his early sixties so there's a probability the strike itself might have precipitated a heart attack. Nevertheless, we'll find that out when we do the post mortem.'

'Is the vase the murder weapon?'

'You'd think it would be, wouldn't you?' said Charles, 'but I doubt it because, as you can see, the skin where he received the blow doesn't appear to be broken. In fact, to be honest, Alistair, I'm mystified as to what the weapon could be, but whatever it is it's not a hard object.'

'Are there any signs of a struggled?' asked Fitzjohn.

'Not on the face of it,' replied Charles as he lifted one of the victim's hands and peered under his finger nails. 'But that also will become clear at the PM.'

'What about the time of death?'

'Ah, finally, a question I can answer with some amount of surety. Firstly, the colour of the bruising on his temple indicates he received the blow in the early hours of this morning. And to back that theory up, his watch is shattered.' Charles lifted up the victim's sleeve to expose his wristwatch, its face smashed. 'It stopped at one a.m. precisely. Having said that, however, we have to take into consideration his body may have functioned for several minutes without oxygen.'

'Even so, one a.m. or a minute or two either way could make all the difference to our investigation into finding the killer,' replied Fitzjohn as the two men got to their feet. 'Anyway, I'll leave you to it for now and see you at the morgue later in the day.'

'And plan to stay for afternoon tea,' said Charles with a smile.

Fitzjohn left the crime scene and carried on through the

warren of dimly lit passageways in search of the auditorium, the only sound that of the floorboards creaking beneath his weight. Before long he found himself in a large open space. Taken aback, he stopped, his eyes squinting as he gazed over a row of footlights into pitch darkness.

'Sir?' Fitzjohn swung around at the sound of Betts' voice. 'You're on the stage, sir.'

'I know that,' replied Fitzjohn with a hiss. 'The problem is, how do I get down?'

'If you walk toward the sound of my voice, you'll find a set of steps.'

Fitzjohn edged forward and moments later, descended into the seating area where a soft hum could be heard coming from the rows filled with people waiting to give their statements. 'I didn't realise there'd be such a crowd,' he said as his eyes adjusted to the light. 'We could be here all day and half the night.'

'There are forty-eight in all, sir. I've called the station and asked for support. In the meantime, I've organised everyone into groups. The director of the play and members of the cast are over to the left, crew members to the far right. The rest of the staff; management, attendants for the snack bar and ticket booth etc., are sitting in the middle.'

'Good man,' replied Fitzjohn as he surveyed the mass of faces. 'What about the lady over there sitting by herself in front of the stage?'

'That's Dolores Madden, sir. She's the person who found Howard Greenwood's body. Apparently, he was the leading man in the play.'

'Is she a member of the cast?' asked Fitzjohn.

'No, sir. She looks after the costume department.'

Fitzjohn took a moment to observe the woman, striking

in her brightly coloured dress and shawl, despite her heavy-set appearance. 'Very well, I'll have a word with her.'

'Ms Madden?' Dolores looked around, her face visibly pale in the dim light. 'I'm DCI Fitzjohn. I'll be conducting the investigation into Howard Greenwood's death. I understand you're the person who found his body this morning.'

'Yes, I am,' replied Dolores, pushing wisps of her dark wavy hair away from her face.

'I appreciate it wasn't an easy encounter for you,' said Fitzjohn aware of the woman's unease. 'Even so, are you able to answer for few questions?'

'I'll try,' replied Dolores her hand trembling as she dabbed her eyes with a tissue. 'Although, I feel a bit muddled. I don't know why.'

'Perhaps if you just give me a brief outline of what happened we can talk further when you've had more time to recover,' Fitzjohn replied as he sat down.

'Okay. I think I can manage that.'

'Very well,' said Fitzjohn. 'To begin with, can you tell me how you came to find the body?'

'Well you see, I'm the costume supervisor. I take care of everything concerning our collection including distribution to the cast. Before last night's performance, I went to see Howard to tell him that one of his costumes for today's matinee wouldn't be available for him to wear. It's being repaired. He was far from pleased, but I assured him I'd find a replacement. That's why I went to his dressing room this morning. To give him the substitute to try on.' Dolores fell silent and closed her eyes. 'I can't get the sight of him out of my mind,' she continued, opening her eyes and staring out over the stage at nothing in particular.

'When you spoke to him last night, how did he seem?' asked Fitzjohn.

'Actually, when I come to think about it, I think I caught him at a bad time, Chief Inspector. You see, his brother, Leo, was with him. I had the feeling I'd interrupted something because they stopped talking as soon as I knocked on the door. It made me feel awkward, so I told Howard about the costume and left.'

'Is his brother also an actor in the play?'

'Far from it. He owns a restaurant in Double Bay. You might have heard of it. It's called The Salty Oyster?'

'I have indeed,' replied Fitzjohn. 'Being that his brother was here early in evening, do you know whether he stayed for the performance?'

'I'm sure he would have because I saw him back stage after the show. Probably to join his brother and the cast in a farewell drink. You see, the theatre is due to close.'

'So I understand,' said Fitzjohn. 'It must be difficult for you and everyone who works here to see that happen.'

'I've worked here now for nearly twenty years, so it is very difficult,' replied Dolores with an air of wistfulness. 'It's the end of an era.'

'How long has the present play been running, Ms Madden?'

'For the past eighteen months.'

'And was Mr Greenwood in his role for that length of time?'

'Yes. It's the original cast but for one person.'

'So, presumably they were a compatible group,' said

Fitzjohn. Dolores did not reply. 'Tell me, Ms Madden, would you say Howard Greenwood was well liked?

'He was initially. Before his wife's death, that is.'

'And when was that?' asked Fitzjohn, his interest piqued.

'It wasn't long after the play opened. Howard became a different person after that, but I suppose it wasn't surprising considering the circumstances. You see, Marsha, that was her name, had been his leading lady in the play. After her death I imagine every performance must have been a painful reminder of her passing.' Dolores paused before she continued. 'Of course, we all tried to make allowances for his grief but as time went by and Howard became increasingly argumentative... Well, let's just say it hasn't been an easy time, Chief Inspector.'

'Who replaced Marsha Greenwood in the leading female role?' asked Fitzjohn.

'Auditions were held and Madelaine Wells, who'd played a minor part previously, was chosen.'

'Is she here this morning?' asked Fitzjohn, looking around.

'I haven't seen her since last night's performance ended.'

'Did she attend the get together after the show?'

'I have no idea since I wasn't invited,' replied Dolores with an indignant tone. 'The party was only for Howard's invited guests and members of the cast.'

'I see. Do you know the names of the guests who were invited, by any chance?'

'Other than Howard's brother, I'm afraid not, Chief Inspector. I'm sorry.'

'Not at all, Ms Madden. You've been most helpful.' Fitzjohn, got to his feet. 'Oh, just one more question, if I may. What time did you leave the theatre last night?'

'It was just as the party got under way. Around eleven-thirty.'

∾

Fitzjohn re-joined Betts in the aisle. 'Have you come across a cast member by the name of Madelaine Wells?' he asked.

'No, sir. There's no one by that name here although Nigel Bennett, the security guard on duty at the stage door last night, did mention her name. Evidently, she became ill during the performance and left soon after the play finished.'

'Which is, no doubt, why she hasn't appeared this morning. Find out whether she called in sick.'

'I have and she did, sir. She spoke to the director of the play early this morning and asked that her understudy take over for the day.'

'Very well. Add her to the list of those we need to locate because even though she didn't attend last night's festivities, we need to speak to her at some point.' Fitzjohn scanned those still seated in the auditorium. 'Has anything come to light while you've been taking statements?' he asked.

'Only that there was a party for the cast after the play finished last night, sir.'

'So Dolores Madden said and confirmed by the glasses and empty champagne bottles scattered around the victim's dressing room. Apparently, it's likely that one of those in attendance was his brother, Leo Greenwood, along with a few other guests. We'll need to find out who they were so we can speak to them,' continued Fitzjohn. 'But for now, there's the pressing matter of informing Howard Greenwood's next of kin of his death and, given his celebrity, I only hope we're able to do so before it's broadcasted throughout the media.

According to Ms Madden, Leo Greenwood, owns a restaurant in Double Bay called "The Salty Oyster" so we'll try there first.'

The two men left the theatre by the stage door and made their way through a soft drizzle of rain, to the car, Fitzjohn dwelling on the unfortunate task ahead.

CHAPTER 4

itzjohn and Betts arrived at The Salty Oyster and walked into the buzz of lunchtime diners. 'Do you have a booking, gentlemen?' asked a voice with a European accent. Brushing off his dampened suit coat, Fitzjohn turned to see a slight man of medium height dressed in a dark suit and carrying a tray of drinks. The plastic tag on his lapel indicated he was Gerard Lafleur, the restaurant's maitre d'.

'No,' replied Fitzjohn. 'We're...'

'In that case, I can only offer you one table towards the back of the restaurant, sir,' continued Gerard, his voice raised above the din.

'That won't be necessary. We're not here to dine.' replied Fitzjohn, 'We're here to speak to Leo Greenwood. Is he available?'

'Are you from the council?' asked the maitre d', his left eyebrow raised as he cast a suspicious eye over the two officers.

'No. We're here to see Mr Greenwood on a personal

matter,' replied Fitzjohn reluctant to display his warrant card amid the diners.

'Is there a problem, Gerard?'

Fitzjohn looked around to see a tall man in his late forties, his small brown eyes and hooked nose set in an angular face. 'These gentlemen wish to speak to you, Leo,' replied Gerard, stepping back.

'If it's a complaint about the food or the service, gentlemen, my maitre d' is the person you should speak to.'

'It's neither, Mr Greenwood. We're here on a purely personal matter.' Feeling Greenwood was not convinced, Fitzjohn finally showed his warrant card.

'The police,' whispered Greenwood under his breath. 'Look, whatever it is, can't you come back in a couple of hours when things here have quietened down. This is our busiest time of the day. I just don't have the time to...'

'I'm sorry, Mr Greenwood but I'm afraid the matter can't wait,' said Fitzjohn. 'We need to speak to you at once.'

'Oh, very well,' said Greenwood with a sigh. 'We can talk in my office. This way.' Fitzjohn and Betts followed Leo's loping stride as they wended their way between the closely arranged tables and chairs into a small room at the rear of the restaurant. 'I didn't realise the council had taken matters this far,' said Leo, gesturing to the chairs in front of his desk before he closed the door and sat down. 'I suppose you're here to serve me a summons.'

'No, Mr Greenwood. We're here to...'

'Oh my god! I'm being sued by one of my diners, aren't I? That's all I need.' Leo slumped back in his chair. 'And even though the health inspector gave us a clean bill of health last week. It doesn't make any sense.'

'We're not here on behalf of the council nor to serve you with a summons. And, as far as I know, you're not being sued,' said Fitzjohn endeavouring to contain his exasperation. 'We're here concerning your brother, Howard. His body was found early this morning in his dressing room at the Adelphi Theatre.'

Leo stared at Fitzjohn with a look of disbelief before he uttered, 'Howard's dead? But I was with him last night. He'd just finished his performance and he was fine. What happened? Was it his heart?'

'All we can tell you at this stage is that we're treating his death as suspicious,' said Fitzjohn.

Leo Greenwood's face paled. 'Suspicious. You mean he was *murdered*? How?'

'He received a blow to the right temple although the actual cause of his death is yet to be determined. I say that because of the possibility that the blow could have precipitated a heart attack, for example.'

'Even so, whoever it was wanted him dead. But why?'

'We had hoped you might be able to shed some light on that,' said Fitzjohn. 'Do you know of anyone your brother had a problem with?'

'That's a difficult question to answer, Chief Inspector, because I should think Howard had a problem with everyone at that theatre. He never stopped complaining about them and I can only think they felt the same way about him because he wasn't an easy person to get along with.'

'You said earlier you were with him after his performance.'

'Yes. You might not be aware, but the Adelphi is being pulled down to make way for inner city apartments. Last night was their last evening performance. Howard asked me to come along and stay for the farewell party he'd organised. To tell you the truth, I can't think why he'd bothered but I guess he had his reasons.' Leo hesitated before he said, 'Did you say he was found in his dressing room?'

'Yes.'

'Which means someone at that gathering killed him, doesn't it?' said Leo.

'Not necessarily,' replied Fitzjohn. 'His assailant might have remained in the theatre and waited until everyone, other than your brother, had left the building.'

'Ah, I see what you mean but under those circumstances it'd be impossible to find his killer. It could be anyone out there.'

'That's true, it could be and it would make our task more difficult but not impossible,' replied Fitzjohn. 'To start with, however, we need to know the people who attended the festivities after the show. Can you tell us who they were?'

'Yes, of course. Let's see, other than myself and members of the cast there was the man who wrote the play, Simon Roach, and the woman who designed the costumes, Stephanie Mowbray.'

'Do you have their contact details by any chance?' asked Fitzjohn.

'No. Being an actor, Howard moved in somewhat different circles than I do. All I can tell you is that Stephanie is a fashion designer. I believe she has a shop in the Strand Arcade in the city and all I know about Simon is that he lives in Cremorne. I'm sorry I can't be of more help, Chief Inspector.'

'That's quite all right, Mr Greenwood. I'm sure we'll be able to contact them both with that information. Do you remember what time you left the theatre, by any chance?'

'It was somewhere around twelve-thirty.'

'And how many people remained when you left?'

'Oh. To be honest, I'd had a few too many glasses of champagne to know for sure although, I do know Stephanie was still there because I said goodbye to her as I left. Simon was there too as was another woman. I don't know who she was but her costume stood out. It was a long electric blue gown with gold beading. I'm afraid that's all can I remember.'

'Thanks, Mr Greenwood. You've been most helpful. I just have one more question. Did you happen to speak to your brother before the performance? The reason I ask is because in hindsight you might remember something he said that would indicate he was troubled.'

'As a matter of fact, I did speak to him; to wish him well. Break a leg as they say.' Leo faltered. 'Anyway, thinking back, the only thing that seemed to be troubling him was the closure of the theatre even though he'd known it was coming for some time.'

Although the rain had ceased, threatening grey clouds obscured the sky and the rumble of distant thunder sounded as Fitzjohn and Betts emerged from The Salty Oyster and walked back to their car.

'Leo Greenwood's interpretation of his discussion with the victim before his performance doesn't match that perceived by Dolores Madden, does it, sir?'

'No, it doesn't, although it is possible that when she came into the room, she took their silence the wrong way,' replied Fitzjohn, 'especially if she and our victim had had words previously over the repairs needed to his costume.' Fitzjohn opened the car door and climbed into the passenger seat. 'Having said that, however, if she's right and they were arguing, I doubt it's something Leo Greenwood would want to admit, given the circumstances.' Fitzjohn sat back and thought for a moment. 'And then there's his description of a blue gown with gold beading worn by one of the party goers. Sounds a lot like the dress Dolores Madden had on this morning, doesn't it? And yet she said she didn't attend the party.'

'Unless there are two such gowns,' said Betts as he pulled out into the traffic.

'It's possible. I suppose a theatre is one place you would find multiple copies of the same garment. Even so, it's something to be noted.'

'Where to now, sir?'

Fitzjohn looked at his watch. 'We'll go to the morgue. Hopefully Charles will have finished the post mortem and have news that will enable us to move forward with our investigation. There's also afternoon tea on offer, I'm told,' Fitzjohn added with a smile.

'I think I'll skip the tea, sir, and find out where Simon Roach can be reached.'

'As you like.'

The antiseptic atmosphere tinged with a metallic tang filled Fitzjohn's nostrils as he followed the attendant through the morgue. From the doorway, Charles Conroy and a technician could be seen going about their tasks. Fitzjohn hovered on the threshold until the pathologist looked up.

'Ah, Alistair. Well timed. We've just finished. Let's go to

my office and I can give you my conclusions while we have that afternoon tea I promised. Betts not with you?' he asked as they left the room.

'He said he preferred to wait in the car and do some background work.'

'Oh. That's a shame because I have chocolate brownies to go with the tea. Still, he's not alone in declining my offer and I don't take it personally. I know it's the venue and not my company that puts folk off,' he added with a chuckle as they reached his office. 'You go in and make yourself comfortable and I'll be right back.'

Moments later, Charles reappeared with a tray containing two steaming cups and a plate of brownies which he placed on the desk before settling himself into his chair. 'Before we get down to business, I have news,' he said, offering Fitzjohn a brownie. 'I'm planning on retiring at the end of winter.'

'Oh,' was all Fitzjohn could manage as he put his cup down.

'You're supposed to say, "That's great, Charles." '

'That's great, Charles, but what will you do to fill your time?'

'I'm planning on moving further up the coast where I can do a bit of fishing and armed with a pair of binoculars, sit on my front porch and watch the whales migrate.'

'It sounds idyllic. I'm jealous,' said Fitzjohn, taking a bite of his brownie.

'Your time will arrive whereas, for me, as I turn seventy in a couple of months, it has arrived.' Charles chose a brownie and sat back with a satisfied smile. 'You'll have to come up for a visit. We can do a bit of fishing.'

'I'll do that,' Fitzjohn replied, finishing his tea.

'Good. Now, let's get down to business,' said Charles, looking down at his notes. 'Firstly, the cause of death was as I suspected, blunt force trauma. There were no signs that the victim suffered either an infarction, in other words a heart attack, or a stroke.'

'So, it was murder,' said Fitzjohn. 'Is there evidence he struggled?'

'No which leads me to think he was taken by complete surprise, although you may have a different view.'

'On the contrary, you're probably right,' said Fitzjohn. 'I doubt he was on his guard as I'm led to believe he was acquainted with everyone who remained in the theatre last night. What about the weapon used? Any thoughts on that? continued Fitzjohn.

'No, and there lies a problem because, at this stage, I have to admit, I'm mystified,' replied Charles. 'It couldn't have been the crystal vase that presumably had held the roses because whatever hit the victim wasn't a hard object. If it had been, there'd be more damage to the skin and as it is, there's only discolouration. What is interesting, however, and isn't visible to the naked eye, is that there are microscopic pieces of plastic lodged in the tissue. I'll have them passed on to the Forensic Services Group for analysis. Hopefully, it'll assist you in finding the murder weapon.'

'And what about time of death? Is that still as you specu-lated at one a.m.?'

'Yes.'

∾

Fitzjohn emerged from the morgue carrying a small brown paper bag. He handed it to Betts as he climbed into the car.

'What's this?' asked Betts, placing his notebook into his inside coat pocket.

'Since you missed lunch and weren't able to join us for afternoon tea, Charles saved a chocolate brownie for you.'

'That was thoughtful of him but...'

'Don't tell me you don't want it just because it came from the morgue. I have it on good authority Charles bought the brownies at the local bakery on his way to work this morning.' Betts peeked inside the bag. 'Come on, Betts. It won't bite you,' said Fitzjohn suppressing a laugh.

'I'll keep it for later, sir.'

'As you wish,' replied Fitzjohn as he pulled his seatbelt on. 'Have you confirmed where Stephanie Mowbray can be contacted and also an address for Simon Roach?'

'I have, sir, and it's as Leo Greenwood said. Stephanie Mowbray does have a shop and workroom for her dress designs in the upper level of the Strand Arcade on George Street and I have an address for Simon Roach in Cremorne.'

'Excellent. We'll speak to Ms Mowbray first.'

CHAPTER 5

itzjohn and Betts entered the Strand Arcade from George Street, its 19th century Victorian architecture of glazed timber shop fronts and ceramic tiled flooring emitting an atmosphere of a time long since passed. Making their way up to the second level, they emerged onto the balcony that stretched around the top floor, its ornamental wrought iron railing enabling a view of the arcade below. Fitzjohn looked up through the glass lantern roof, the heavy dark clouds a reminder of the blustery day outside before he continued on to where Betts stood in front of one of the shopfronts. It was unadorned but for a window display of the type of clothes that could be anticipated inside, and the plate glass window overlaid with the words, "Stephanie Mowbray Fashion Designs" in bold gold lettering. The two officers entered the shop to the tinkle of a small bell hung on the back of the door. Fitzjohn took in the room edged with racks of colourful dresses, scarves, and shelving filled with hats, soft leather handbags and gloves before his gaze came to rest on a vase of long-stemmed red roses on the counter. At that same moment, a tall, dark-haired woman probably in her mid-forties with large tortoise shell framed glasses perched on her long-pointed nose, emerged from the back room. Wearing a slim fitting purple dress, its length almost hiding her black stockinged legs, she glided across the floor.

'Can I help you?' she asked, peering closely at the two officers.

'We're from the police, madam,' said Fitzjohn. 'Are you Stephanie Mowbray?'

'Yes, I am. Are you here concerning Howard Greenwood, by any chance? It's just that I heard about what happened to him only minutes ago, on the news.'

'We are.' Fitzjohn held up his warrant card and introduced himself and Betts. 'We're investigating the circumstances in which he died.'

'You mean it wasn't by natural causes? I thought perhaps... That is, I know he had high blood pressure.'

'I'm afraid Mr Greenwood was attacked by person or persons unknown in the early hours of this morning at the Adelphi Theatre,' replied Fitzjohn.

'Oh. But who would want to do that to him?'

'We understand Mr Greenwood hosted a party after last night's performance.'

'That's right, he did. I was there. He called it a wake because the theatre is being demolished. An innocuous term to use at the time but now...' Stephanie hesitated. 'I'm sorry it's just such a shock,' she continued, her voice quavering.

A moment of silence followed before Fitzjohn asked, 'I know it's a difficult time, Ms Mowbray, but it might help us to know who else attended the party?'

'Yes, of course. Well, let me think. They were mainly

members of the cast. The only non-actors were Howard's brother, Leo, Simon Roach who wrote the play and me, of course.'

'Are you well acquainted with both Leo Greenwood and Simon Roach?' asked Fitzjohn.

'No, not really. I've met Leo a couple of times when I've dined at one of his restaurants, but Simon Roach I'd only met once before at a Christmas party that Howard and his wife Marsha hosted.'

'I see. And how long had you known the Greenwoods?' asked Fitzjohn.

'Oh, we go back a long way. Before I got into fashion design, I tried acting. The three of us were students together at acting school. Howard and Marsha went on, of course, to have successful careers whereas I decided it wasn't for me. We stayed in touch though. Marsha wore a lot of my designs.' Stephanie smiled. 'They were the perfect couple. Both loved the theatrical life until, sadly, Marsha died. I don't think Howard ever got over it. He worshipped her; he really did.'

'We understand Mrs Greenwood died at a Christmas party. Was that the same Christmas party where you met Simon Roach?'

'Yes, as a matter of fact, it was. It was a heartbreaking evening.'

'Did you witness the incident, Ms Mowbray?'

'Thankfully no. I was outside on the patio at the time. There was panic initially, as I remember but good sense prevailed, and an ambulance was called. The paramedics did what they could, but I understand she died on her way to the hospital.'

As Stephanie spoke, the bell on the door tinkled and a woman walked in. 'Oh, this is my two-p.m. fitting.'

'In that case, before we leave,' said Fitzjohn, 'can you tell us what time you left the party last night?'

'Yes. It was just before midnight. The party had barely got underway but I had a client arriving early this morning so I couldn't stay any longer.'

'Did anyone else leave at the same time?'

'No. As I said, the party was just getting underway.'

'So you were the first to leave?'

'I think so, yes.' Stephanie smiled before glancing at her client. 'Will that be all, Chief Inspector?'

'Yes, other than to ask about the roses on your counter over there. Can you tell me how you came by them? A gift from a friend, perhaps?'

Stephanie looked over her shoulder. 'Funny you should ask. I suppose they are a gift of sorts, but not from a friend. I must have a secret admirer because they were lying in front of the door when I arrived this morning.'

'No card with them?' asked Fitzjohn.

'No.'

The two officers left Stephanie Mowbray in conversation with her client and emerged from the arcade into the rain swept afternoon. Buffeted by the wind, Fitzjohn pulled up the collar of his raincoat and, following Betts, dashed across the street to the car.

'Leo Greenwood seemed positive that Stephanie Mowbray was still at the party when he left and yet she appears certain she was the first to leave,' said Betts as he turned the windshield wipers on and pulled out into the traffic.

'Well, Greenwood did say he'd had a few too many glasses of champagne so his memory may not be serving him well. Still, it'll be interesting to hear what Simon Roach has to say,' said Fitzjohn, settling himself back in the passenger seat. 'To tell you the truth, it's the roses on the counter that worry me,' he continued. 'Either it's a disturbing coincidence that a secret admirer decided to leave Ms Mowbray flowers on this particular morning or they're from our killer in which case she may be in danger.'

'Or she had something to do with Greenwood's death and she sees the flowers as a way of deflecting suspicion from herself,' replied Betts.

'That's a good point and it's a possibility we have to consider,' said Fitzjohn as they crossed the harbour bridge onto the north side of the city. As they did so, the two men fell into silence as Betts manoeuvred his way through the traffic. When they reached Cremorne, he slowed down before he pulled over in front of a Federation style house, its front garden enclosed behind a white wooden fence where geraniums and rose bushes had entangled themselves between the palings. Fitzjohn swept an admiring glance over the garden as they walked to the front door where he rang the bell. Presently, the door opened to reveal a tall, slightly built man with curly dark brown hair, wearing a turtleneck sweater and jeans.

'Mr Roach?' said Fitzjohn, stepping forward.

'Yes. I'm Simon Roach. And you are?'

'We're from the police, sir,' replied Fitzjohn, showing his warrant card. 'We're conducting an investigation into the death of a man by the name of Howard Greenwood whom we understand you were acquainted.'

'I was, yes. For the past eighteen months, Howard has

played the lead role in a play I wrote some time ago. My agent phoned about an hour ago to tell me he died last night at the theatre. I'm finding it difficult to believe, particularly since I attended a party Howard hosted after the show.'

'So we understand and that's why we'd like to speak to you. May we come in?'

'Yes, of course, come through, gentlemen.' Roach stepped back from the door before leading the way along a wide hall, the aged oak floor boards creaking under their weight. The warmth emanating from a log fire in the living room met them as they entered. 'Please, make yourselves comfortable,' he said, gesturing to the leather armchairs that encircled the fireplace. 'On cold, wet days such as this, I like to have a fire burning while I work.' As he spoke he looked towards his desk set in the bay window. 'Now, how can I help?' he asked, joining them by the fire.

'With regard to the party you attended last night, how did Howard Greenwood seem at the time?' asked Fitzjohn as he settled himself into one of the leather armchairs.

'I think he was like all of us, saddened by the imminent closer of the theatre but other than that, he appeared his usual self. You have to understand, Chief Inspector, Howard was a rather sober fellow. He was never the life of any party. Even so, he was pleasant enough because I'm sure he felt that, as the leading man, it was his responsibility to offer the cast some sort of farewell get-together.'

'Did you get on well with him?' asked Fitzjohn.

'To be honest, I can't say I did. At least not since the death of his wife, Marsha. Do you know about that?'

'We do,' replied Fitzjohn. 'We understand she died during a party at their home some time ago. Were you there at the time?'

'I was,' replied Simon. 'Such a tragic thing to happen. She was a talented actress. And it begs belief how Howard carried on in the role without her. I could never understand why he persisted because his grief did cause problems in his interactions with the other actors. Disharmony is a lethal ingredient when you're putting on a production.'

'No doubt,' said Fitzjohn. 'And with that in mind, are you aware of anyone who was particularly affected by Mr Greenwood's unfortunate behaviour?' As Simon did not respond to the question, Fitzjohn quickly added, 'No matter how insignificant it may seem.'

'Well, I don't know if it was a result of his grief, but he did have a particular dislike for a woman by the name of Dolores Madden. She worked at the Adelphi as the costume director. They clashed constantly so I'm told. He believed her to be incompetent to the point of asking the theatre management to have her replaced.' As he spoke, Simon rose from his chair and, taking the poker, tended to the logs in the fire. 'She remained on staff, however, so I daresay his request fell on deaf ears.'

'I see. Anything else?' asked Fitzjohn.

Roach thought for a moment before he said, 'Well, I may be mistaken, of course, but on a personal front I think Howard had been going through a bit of a rough patch with his brother and knowing Leo, I can only imagine it had something to do with money. I say that because of the odd comments he had made over the years of our acquaintance. It seemed to me that his brother leaned heavily on him.'

'I see,' said Fitzjohn. 'What time did you leave the party, Mr Roach?'

'I think it was around twelve-thirty.'

'Were you the first to leave?' asked Fitzjohn.

'That's hard to say in the crush of that small dressing room.'

'That being so, can you remember who remained?'

'There were quite a few members of the cast still there and I can't be certain but Howard's brother, Leo, might have been there also.'

'Can you name the cast members?'

'I'm afraid I wasn't taking that much notice although I think I saw Madelaine Wells in the laneway as I left the building. She played the leading female role opposite Howard.'

'Well, I think that's about all for now,' said Fitzjohn, getting to his feet. 'Thank you for your time.'

'Not at all, Chief Inspector,' replied Simon as he led the way back to the front door. 'I just hope I've been of some help.'

'Everything helps in some way,' said Fitzjohn with a quick smile. 'We'll be in touch if we find we have any more questions. Oh, there is one thing. When you left the theatre did you come straight home?'

'Yes. I arrived home at about a quarter past one this morning.'

'Can anyone verify that?'

'I doubt it. I live here alone.'

'Well, according to Simon Roach, Leo Greenwood might still have been at the party at around twelve-thirty,' said Betts as they emerged from the house. 'One of them is mistaken or lying.'

'It's possible but Greenwood also told us that he said

goodbye to Stephanie Mowbray on his way out of the dressing room and if she is to be believed, she'd already left the theatre,' Fitzjohn replied buffeted by the wind as he climbed into the passenger seat of the car. 'What's also interesting is the fact that both Mowbray and Roach were at the Christmas party where Marsha Greenwood died. It tends to give weight to a notion that one or both of them could be involved in Howard Greenwood's death, doesn't it? After all, neither have alibis. Either one could have snuck back into the theatre until everyone had left.'

'I can see that they both had the opportunity but there's still motive to consider and the means,' said Betts. 'After all, Charles Conroy hasn't come up with a murder weapon yet?'

'Mmm. Add them both to our background checks, Betts, as well as that cast member Simon Roach mentioned.'

'Madelaine Wells?'

'Yes. We'll speak to her next but for now, let's get to the station. We have to organise a management meeting as soon as possible.'

'I spoke to Williams earlier, sir, while you were in the morgue. He should have it all set up by the time we arrive.'

CHAPTER 6

itzjohn and Betts walked into the station to be met by the duty officer who looked at Betts questionably. However, it was Fitzjohn, eager to impede further speculation relating to his presumed relationship with Peta Ashby, who addressed the sergeant. 'Good morning, Sergeant. You're just the man I want to see.'

'Good morning, sir,' replied the duty officer, his eyes darting back in Betts' direction.

'You don't need to look at Betts because I can answer your question,' continued Fitzjohn. 'You lost the bet. Chief Superintendent Ashby could not be found at my home. Consequently, I'm sure you'll see to it that those who did make money on your little venture will donate it to the station's charity fund. It won't make you popular, but it will ensure you have been instrumental in doing something worthwhile with your time.' As the duty officer's face reddened, Fitzjohn gave a quick smile, turned and carried on to his office but not without noticing the shrug given to the duty officer by Betts.

Satisfied he had got his point across, Fitzjohn walked into his office and placed his briefcase on his desk but as he sat down, he looked up to see Peta Ashby in the doorway.

'Good afternoon, Fitzjohn,' she said with a warm smile that somewhat softened the embodiment of officialdom her uniformed attire presented.

'Good afternoon, ma'am,' replied Fitzjohn, scrambling to his feet and at the same time endeavouring to suppress the feeling of attraction that welled up inside him. In a flash, the wager that had involved them both crossed his mind. Should he mention it to her? he asked himself as he offered her a chair. Would it serve any purpose, especially since he had decided not to pursue their friendship further than that of chance meetings at the Charlotte Café? Granted there was no rule against fraternisation in the department, but it could lead to difficulties demonstrated by this morning's performance. It was clear that tongues had wagged so obviously his feelings toward the chief superintendent were not as discrete as he may have wished. He had to make sure that didn't happen again.

'How did everything go at the crime scene this morning?' asked Peta as she settled herself into a chair.

'Interesting to say the least,' said Fitzjohn, the long-stemmed red roses coming to mind once again. 'I'll be holding a management meeting on the details in a few minutes.'

'In that case, I'll attend.' Peta started to get up but hesitated.

'Is there something else, ma'am?'

'No, it can wait until later.' As she spoke, Betts appeared in the doorway. 'Hello, Sergeant,' she said with a smile.

'Ma'am.' As the chief superintendent disappeared through the doorway Betts sighed. 'She never fails to notice me and say hello. It makes me feel visible.'

From where he stood behind his desk, Fitzjohn craned his neck upwards. 'Believe me, Betts, with your height you're impossible to miss.'

Fitzjohn entered the incident room to the low hum of voices that dissipated as he joined Betts next to the whiteboard.

'Good afternoon all,' he said, adjusting his wire-framed glasses and casting his eye over the plain-clothed and uniformed officers gathered before him. As he did so, the door at the rear of the room opened and Peta walked in unobtrusively standing against the back wall. Nevertheless, it did not pass Fitzjohn's notice that several of those present turned and nudged each other which only reinforced his earlier decision. 'We have what I think will be a particularly complex investigation so plenty of work for you all to get involved in,' he continued before turning to the whiteboard.

'The victim is a fifty-nine-year-old male by the name of Howard Greenwood. You might recognise the name as he was a well-known thespian.' A number of blank faces looked back at him. 'In other words, he was an actor. His body was found at approximately nine-forty this morning in his dressing room at the Adelphi Theatre where a party had been held the previous evening. The post mortem has confirmed his death occurred at approximately one a.m. Cause of death blunt force trauma. The weapon used, however, has not as yet been identified. To help us in that regard, the forensic pathologist has detected minute traces of plastic in the wound site here on the temple.' Fitzjohn pointed to a photograph of the victim displayed on the whiteboard. 'As we speak forensics are conducting an analysis in order to ascertain the type of plastic involved. Hopefully, the result will assist us in finding the murder weapon. As you can see, a number of persons of interest have been identified,' he continued, drawing attention to a list of names. 'These include members of the cast who attended the party along with three invited guests. The victim's brother, Leo Greenwood, Stephanie Mowbray, a dress designer of some note and Simon Roach, a playwright and author of the play being performed. I would like to add, however, that it is not beyond the bounds of possibility that the killer was not amongst those at the party but waited elsewhere in the theatre until an opportunity arose.'

'What about motive for the killing, sir?' asked one of the young constables.

'Although it appears there was friction between the victim and his fellow actors, as yet, a motive has not been established. Any more questions?' Fitzjohn asked looking around the room. When silence prevailed he said, 'Right, we'll start with the usual background and telephone checks and continue our search for the murder weapon at the theatre. This will be made easier by the fact that the theatre has now been closed until its demolition in the near future. DS Betts will hand out your assignments before you leave. Thank you all and good luck.'

As those attending the meeting gathered around Betts at the whiteboard, Fitzjohn joined Peta Ashby as she left the room.

'It doesn't sound like you have much to go on,' she said.

'We don't, but hopefully when the background checks are complete, something will come to light.' Fitzjohn paused as they reached Peta's office doorway. 'Earlier, it seemed that there was something you wanted to talk to me about.'

'Ah, so there was. Just a slight problem but I resolved it,' Peta replied with a quick smile. 'Keep me up to date with your investigation as you go along, won't you, Fitzjohn?'

'Yes, ma'am.'

CHAPTER 7

*C*onstance Parsons, with her diminutive frame enveloped in a dark blue winter coat, tightened her woollen scarf around her neck against the cold as she emerged from St Leonard's train station. It was silly of me to stay at the bookshop so late on such a night, she thought as she descended the steps into a fine mist that hung low in the air. This thought grew in significance when she reached the empty taxi rank and looked around the street now almost deserted of pedestrians. What was I thinking? For a short time, she stood and waited for a cab but as the minutes ticked by and the dampness started to penetrate her coat, she gave a sigh, turned and started to walk away from the lights of the station and along the dimly lit footpath towards her home at the top of the rise. At least walking will be warmer than standing here any longer, she told herself.

Strangely enough, despite the cold night the scent of flowers wafted in the air from the gardens as she passed by. So absorbed was she in their diverse fragrances as well as the thought of the hot cocoa she planned to make when she arrived home, that she failed to notice the sound of footsteps that kept pace with her stride. Until, that is, she stopped to cross the road and became aware of an unexpected silence. Gingerly, she turned and peered along the darkened street. With no one in sight, she berated herself for letting her imagination run riot and continued on until she reached the familiar low iron gate that led into her front garden. The hinges squeaked as it swung open. Not bothering to close the gate behind her, she fumbled in her handbag for her door key and, on reaching the porch ran up the steps anxious to get into the warmth. As the door swung open, she stepped inside and gave a sigh, at the same time glancing over her shoulder, a sense of doubt at the fringes of her mind. Had there been someone there? Shaking off the thought, she went to close the door but as she did she gave an involuntary gasp when a shadowy figure near the gate moved. I was right, someone was following me, she thought as she slammed the door and turned the deadlock. Without switching on the hall light, she made her way through the darkened house to the kitchen where she threw her handbag onto the table and closed the blinds against the blackness on the other side of the glass. 'Perhaps the cocoa will help calm me down,' she mumbled as she switched on the light. 'And some music wouldn't go amiss.' An old favourite melody calmed her as she stood at the kitchen counter stirring the steaming brew. As she did so, however, the music ceased, interrupted by breaking news. Even the clatter of the spoon when it hit the tiled floor did not take her attention away from the news reader's steady voice as he told of Howard Greenwood's murder.

'Murdered!' A cold shiver ran down her spine and the shadowy figure at the gate came back to mind. As she dwelt on this thought, her last hint of composure deserted her when the doorbell rang. With a degree of uncertainty, she left the kitchen and walked back along the unlit hallway to the front door. There, she hesitated and flinched when the bell rang again.

'Constance, it's Harriet,' came a voice.

'*Harriet*! Thank heavens.' With a surge of relief, she released the deadlock and flung open the door to see Harriet's, large frame all but hidden inside her winter coat against the cold.

'All your lights are out so for a moment there I thought you weren't home,' she said as she bustled inside. 'Had you forgotten I said I'd pick you up for our bridge evening at Pamela's?'

'No, I hadn't forgotten,' Constance lied, her eyes darting past her friend to the street beyond before she closed and locked the door. 'I was a bit late getting home this evening, that's all. Come through to the kitchen. I've just made some cocoa. Would you like a cup?'

'That would be nice. It might warm me up a bit.' In the kitchen, Harriet pulled out a chair and sat down at the large oak table in the centre of the room. 'You must be upset about the state of your roses along your front fence.'

'Upset? Why should I be upset?' asked Constance as she brought two steaming cups of cocoa to the table.

'Because it looks like someone's taken the secateurs to them. Their blooms are all over the sidewalk. Didn't you notice when you arrived home?'

'No because they were all attached to the rose bushes when I got here.' Constance pulled out a chair and sat down. 'Did you see anyone outside,' she asked.

'No. I must have frightened whoever it was when I drove

up. Why would someone do such a thing. A jealous neighbour?'

'I can only think it was the person who followed me home from the station tonight,' said Constance.

'*Followed you?*' screeched Harriet wide eyed.

'Yes, although I didn't realise it until I got here.'

'Oh, Constance. That's frightening. I thought you looked a bit on edge the minute you opened the front door.'

'I doubt it's the only reason. Just before you arrived, I heard on the radio that Howard Greenwood has been murdered.'

'*Murdered?*' Harriet's eyes grew round. 'But why? Was it a random attack?'

'They gave very little detail, only that he was found earlier today at the theatre.'

'Oh. I am sorry,' said Harriet sitting back in her chair. 'I never met the man, but I know you and he have been working closely together for months on his memoir. No wonder you look pale. Just as well it's our bridge night. What I mean is, a bit of company at a time like this is what you need, Constance.'

'I'm sorry, Harriet, but I can't play bridge this evening because there's something I need to do.'

'Due to his death, you mean?'

'Yes.'

'Wouldn't it be better to leave it till morning?'

'No. You see, I need to talk to the police and the sooner I do so, the better.'

'Do you think it's wise to involve yourself, Constance?' asked Harriet with a grimace. 'After all, he has been murdered.'

'I know but I'm sure the police will seek me out during

the course of their investigation anyway, and besides, I owe it to Howard to tell them what I know whether it helps or not.'

'What exactly do you know?' asked Harriet, her inquisitive side piqued.

'I'd rather not say,' replied Constance, gathering the cups and placing them in the sink.

'Is it because you know who murdered him?' prompted Harriet.

'Of course not, but whoever did, might...'

Harriet's face paled. 'Come after you next, you mean? Oh, Constance, it's why you were followed this evening, isn't it?'

'Not necessarily.'

'Have you ever been inside a police station before, Constance?' asked Harriet as they arrived at the station and she pulled into the parking area.

'No, I haven't.'

'Neither have I but I'm more than happy to come in with you. After all, who knows what you might be exposed to in there at this time of night. Criminals no less.'

'Thanks for offer, Harriet, but I'm sure I'll be fine. It is a police station after all.'

While Harriet waited in the car, Constance walked inside and approached a counter situated behind a sheet of glass. Bullet proof no doubt, she thought as she waited for someone to materialise from the inner door. As that thought sprang to mind a tall uniformed officer came into view.

'Good evening, madam, can I help you?'

'Yes,' replied Constance looking up at the towering,

youthful, figure. 'I know it's late, but I'd like to speak to one of your detectives, if he's still here, that is. I have his name written down,' she continued, unfolding the piece of paper in her hand. 'His name is Detective Chief Inspector Fitzjohn.'

'Can I ask what it's in relation to, madam?'

'It's about Howard Greenwood's murder. I have information that I believe the Chief Inspector should be made aware of.'

'Very well, if you'd care to take a seat, I'll see if he's still in the building.'

'As the officer left, Constance turned and scrutinised the sparsely furnished reception area before she settled herself on one of the grey plastic chairs against the far wall. Moments later, a door into what she imagined was the inner sanctum opened and a man in his mid-fifties, impeccably dressed in a finely tailored dark grey suit and maroon tie, crossed the floor towards her with an air of friendly congeniality.

'Ms Parsons,' he said with a smile as he offered his hand. 'I'm DCI Fitzjohn. I understand you wish to speak to me in relation to the Howard Greenwood case.'

'Yes, I do, Chief Inspector,' replied Constance, getting to her feet. 'I don't know if what I have to say will help in any way but, even so, I thought I should come to see you.'

'And I appreciate it, especially considering the conditions outside. So if you'd care to come this way, we can talk in my office.'

Constance followed the chief inspector through the door from which he had emerged and into an atmosphere humming with activity, despite the hour. A place that never sleeps, she thought, her eyes darting around as she followed him into his office.

'This is Detective Sergeant Betts, Ms Parsons,' said the chief inspector. 'He'll be working closely with me on the case.' The tall, ginger-haired young man the chief inspector was referring to scrambled to his feet and offered Constance a chair.

'Thank you, Sergeant,' she said as they each sat down. 'As I told the Chief Inspector, I'm unsure whether what I have to say will be of any assistance to you, but I thought I should come in all the same. And I would have been here sooner, but I didn't hear the news about Howard until this evening when I arrived home from work. It's been such a shock,' she continued as she removed her leather gloves.

'Are you related to Mr Greenwood?' asked the chief inspector.

'No. I knew Howard only as the ghost writer of his memoir.'

'Oh?' The chief inspector sat forward in his chair, his interest piqued.

'Yes. We've been working on the manuscript for the past six months. Of course, I have no idea whether it'll help with your investigation but I thought it's something you should know about. If you don't already, that is.'

'As a matter of fact, no one we've spoken to so far has mentioned it,' said the chief inspector, 'so I'm very pleased you've come in, Ms Parsons. As you're no doubt aware, every piece of information we can gather will help our investigation in one way or another. Is the manuscript complete?'

'It is but for the last chapter which we were to discuss tomorrow, as a matter of fact.'

'I see. Did Mr Greenwood give you any hint as to what he planned for that last chapter?'

'Yes, he did,' replied Constance. 'He said it would centre

on his wife Marsha's murder and although he didn't plan on naming names, in the right hands, the book would guarantee her killer would be brought to justice.'

'You say her murder and yet we're led to believe that according to the coroner's finding, his wife died accidentally when she fell down a flight of stairs at their home in Mosman.'

'That's right but it became clear to me during writing the manuscript that Howard didn't agree with the coroner,' said Constance.

'Is that so?' The chief inspector sat in thought for a moment before he said, 'In his memoir, does Mr Greenwood give any indication why he felt as he did?'

'There are a few obscure inferences but that's about all. I believe he was keeping his more damning accusations for the end.'

'Tell me, Ms Parsons. How much of this manuscript concerns his wife and her death?'

'I'd say her story is woven throughout. It's almost as though you're reading Marsha's biography. I did try on several occasions to steer him in the direction of his own life and achievements, but he wouldn't have it. You see, he was fixated with finding her killer.'

'Was it common knowledge he was writing a memoir? Amongst those he associated with, that is?' asked the chief inspector.

'I have a feeling his brother, Leo, might have known about it but I doubt he would have told anyone else, especially the folk at the theatre. After all, he believed one of them killed his wife. Having said that, however, since we usually held our meetings at the theatre where Howard spent most of his time. I'm sure my comings and goings caused a certain amount of curiosity amongst the cast and crew, so it's possible the people there drew their own conclusions.'

Constance paused. 'I feel rather foolish now because all along I thought his assumption about her death was driven by grief. With what's happened to him, however, I'm beginning to wonder if he was right.'

'In relation to the manuscript itself, Ms Parsons. How many copies are there?'

'Ah. I thought you'd ask that, so I brought them with me,' replied Constance. 'A hard copy and an electronic copy.' Constance opened her briefcase and took out a thick wad of paper held together by two rubber bands along with a USB flash drive which she placed on the chief inspector's desk.

'Did Mr Greenwood also keep a copy?' asked the chief inspector as he picked up the manuscript.

'No,' replied Constance. 'Our routine was that I gave him a chapter to read through and edit after which he returned it to me the next time we met. His instructions were always verbal although he may have made notes which, I suppose, raises the question. If the killer's motive did concern the manuscript and he didn't get what he wanted from Howard, am I the next target?' The shadowy figure standing in her garden and the vandalised roses came into Constance's mind.

'I don't wish to alarm you Ms Parsons, but it can't be discounted,' replied the chief inspector, his hand now resting on the manuscript. 'You are privy to its content whether or not it's in your possession. However, it is highly possible that the coroner's finding is correct and Mr Greenwood's murder was precipitated by something quite apart from his wife's death.' The chief inspector paused for a moment before he asked, 'Even so, to be on the safe side, have you family or a friend you can stay with for the next few days? Just until we've determined the motive behind his killing.'

'I do have a very dear friend I could stay with, but I can't hide away, Chief Inspector. I have my business to consider and winter is my busiest time of year. I can't afford to close, even for a day.'

'What line of business are you in, Ms Parsons?'

'I have a bookshop called "The Next Page Bookshop", in Crows Nest. My foray into ghost writing is a new venture. It's something I thought I might like to do full-time when I retire.' Constance chuckled. 'I shouldn't laugh but it never dawned on me it could involve murder.'

Constance emerged from the police station and re-joined Harriet in the car. 'I'm sorry I took so long,' she said, settling herself into the passenger seat.

'Were you able to speak to the detective in charge of the case?' asked Harriet, her inquisitive nature stirred.

'Yes. Detective Chief Inspector Alistair Fitzjohn is his name and, I must say, I was quite surprised.'

'Pleasantly or otherwise?' asked Harriet.

'Pleasantly. For a start, he was particularly well groomed. Not something I expected in his line of work. He even wore a handkerchief in his breast pocket that matched his tie. You don't often see that nowadays, do you, Harriet? But perhaps more importantly, I think he's probably an exceptional detective. At least that's the impression I got.'

'Did you tell him you were followed on your way home from the station this evening? And about your roses being decimated.'

'No, I didn't mention that.'

'But why not?' asked Harriet aghast.

'I couldn't see the point because I have no idea what the person looked like,' replied Constance. 'He was just a shadow in my garden. And besides, he probably had nothing to do with Howard's murder.'

'But what if he did and you there alone in the house tonight. I think you should come and stay at my place. Just until the police have caught the killer.'

'I do appreciate the offer, Harriet, I really do, but there's no point hiding myself away. After all, I spend my days in the bookshop where anyone can walk in off the street. And besides, I'm rarely there alone. There's a constant stream of customers browsing through the books most of the day.'

'That's not the same as being at home alone in the middle of the night,' replied Harriet. 'In that situation you'd be defenceless. And as far as the bookshop is concerned, one of those customers could be Howard Greenwood's killer. Don't you think it might be wise to close the shop for the time being?'

'I can't do that. I have orders to fill not to mention a dozen or so searches I'm conducting for several customers who are waiting for rare and out-of-print books.'

'That's no excuse for putting yourself at risk,' replied Harriet, shaking her head as she started the car and pulled away from the curb.

'I know you mean well, Harriet, but I'll be fine. Really I will.'

'All right,' replied Harriet with a degree of exasperation. 'But if you change your mind my offer still stands. You're more than welcome to come and stay with me for as long as you wish.'

'I'll keep that in mind,' said Constance, reluctant to accept Harriet's offer since it could put her life in danger also.

'I happen not to be working tomorrow,' said Harriet, filling the void of silence as they drove. 'I could spend the day with you at the bookshop. I know it's only the one day, but you've had a terrible shock with what's happened to Howard so, other than keeping you company, I'm sure I can be of some use.'

CHAPTER 8

While Betts escorted Constance Parsons outside to her waiting car, Fitzjohn had copies of the manuscript run-off and then returned to his office. Hopefully, these pages will contain a clue as to why Howard Greenwood was so brutally murdered and whether or not it had anything to do with his wife's death, he thought with a surge of optimism as he sat down at his desk. At that moment, Betts came back into the office. 'Were you able to convince Ms Parsons to stay with her friend?' he asked.

'I don't think so, sir. I got the impression she thinks it could bring trouble to her friend's door if something should happen.'

'But that would only happen if her whereabouts were known. Having said that, however, I can see her point.' Fitzjohn took his glasses off, set them down on the desk and sat back in his chair. 'Even so, I do wish she'd heeded my advice but all we can do is make the suggestion. And as far as this manuscript is concerned, I wonder if Leo Greenwood knows about it.'

'If he does, you'd think he'd have mentioned it to us,' said Betts as he sat down.

'You'd think so, but as we had just informed him of his brother's death, I doubt his thoughts were clear. So it's probably not surprising,' replied Fitzjohn. 'Any news on the murder weapon?'

'I had a team comb the theatre late this afternoon, sir, but they didn't find anything. They'll continue in the morning.'

'Good.' Fitzjohn looked at his watch. 'I think we should call it a day, don't you?' he said as he placed one copy of the manuscript into his briefcase and closed the lid.

'You're not thinking of reading that tonight are you sir? It's already after eleven o'clock.'

'Needs must, Betts. I had a copy made for you too while you were seeing Ms Parsons out so you can do the same.' A groan left Betts' lips. 'It shouldn't take you more than a couple of hours. We can discuss our findings, if any, in the morning.' With a chuckle, Fitzjohn shrugged into his overcoat, switched off the light and, followed by Betts, left his office.

When he emerged from the station, the storm clouds moved swiftly across a full moon, its brightness defused into a milky glow. Fitzjohn settled himself into the back seat of the waiting cab, his mind awash with the events of the day. Adding to this, when at last the taxi pulled up in front of his cottage in the leafy suburban street of Birchgrove, he heaved a sigh when he noticed the glow of an internal light through the stained glass sections of the front door. This can only mean that Meg is here, unannounced as usual, he thought.

Hoping she had retired for the evening, he opened the front door and stepped inside as the clock on the mantelpiece in the living room struck midnight.

'Is that you, Alistair?' came his sister's voice from upstairs.

'Yes, Meg. No need to get up. We'll talk in the morning.'

'But you won't have time in the morning,' she replied, descending the stairs in her dressing gown, her greying hair in curlers. 'You'll be off to the station before I've barely woken up and its imperative I speak to you about Sophie.'

'But it's midnight and I have reading to do before I go to bed,' he replied, walking through to the kitchen where he shrugged out of his overcoat, loosened his tie and removed the manuscript from his briefcase.

'Whatever it is it can't be as important as your niece's future,' said Meg, following his every move.

'This isn't about Sophie and Martin Betts moving in together, is it?' asked Fitzjohn, turning to face his sister.

'You know about it and you didn't think to tell me?'

'I assumed you knew,' replied Fitzjohn.

'How would I know? Sophie doesn't tell me anything. I rely on you, Alistair, to keep me informed about what's going on in her life.'

'The decision was only made the other day. I'm sure she plans to tell you.'

'And I'll tell her I'm against the idea.'

'Meg, you don't have any say in the matter,' replied Fitzjohn in exasperation. 'Sophie is more than capable of making her own decisions. In other words, it's none of your business.'

'*Alistair Fitzjohn*, you've never spoken to me like that before in your life. I'm shocked.'

'I should have done so a long time ago for your own sake

as well as your daughter's,' Fitzjohn heard himself saying. 'And since I've started, I may as well continue. You can give your daughter advice if she asks for it but otherwise you have to support her in her life's choices, not put road blocks in her way because eventually you'll drive her away. You don't want that, do you, Meg.?'

'I'm her mother. I have a responsibility to make sure she doesn't do something she'll regret later on.'

'That's where you're wrong,' replied Fitzjohn. 'Sophie is no longer a child. She's a grown woman who is starting her career in forensic science and happens to be in love with my sergeant whom she plans to marry. She's happy. You should be pleased for her.'

'They're putting the cart before the horse, Alistair, and you know it. They should get married first.' An awkward silence descended on the kitchen before Meg turned and stormed out of the room.

I've really done it this time, thought Fitzjohn as he watched her go, aware his words had created a schism between them that might never be resolved. Disheartened, he walked into the conservatory and sat down heavily into a chair, removed the rubber bands that held the manuscript together and began to read.

Fitzjohn rose later than usual the following morning, his thoughts a mixture of what the manuscript had revealed about Howard Greenwood's life and how he could repair the damage his words had caused between himself and his sister the night before. As he left his bedroom, he was aware of the silence in the house, a rare event while Meg was in residence.

With a suspicion she might have returned to Melbourne without a word, he glanced through the guestroom doorway as he passed by. With her suitcase in plain sight, he gave a sigh of relief and made his way downstairs to the kitchen where he found Meg standing at the window with her back to him, looking out over the garden.

'Good morning, Meg.' His sister turned, a pained look across her face. 'I can understand if you've taken offence at what I said to you last night. I just don't want to see a rift develop between you and your daughter, that's all.'

'Do you know when she's moving into the apartment?'

'It's this coming weekend,' replied Fitzjohn.

'Then perhaps I could help her,' said Meg.

Knowing how difficult it must be for his sister to give way to a new perspective, Fitzjohn smiled. 'I'm sure she'd appreciate that. Now, I just want to check on the orchids before I leave for the station.'

'What about breakfast?' asked Meg.

'I'll get something at the canteen.'

'That's not good enough, Alistair. You really must take better care of your diet.' Meg hesitated. 'On second thought, I'm sure you know best.'

Taken by surprise at this response as well as encouraged that his sister might have taken his words to heart, Fitzjohn said, 'Would you like to come down to the greenhouse with me? I'd really appreciate your opinion on which orchid I should bench at the next orchid society meeting.'

'I doubt I'd be much help, Alistair. I know nothing about orchids.'

'But you are able to tell me which plant appeals to you the most. How about it?'

'Well, I suppose I can do that,' replied Meg.

With the mood lifted, Fitzjohn led the way down the garden path and into the greenhouse. When they emerged half an hour later, Meg carried the chosen specimen with pride. 'You know, I think I might take up orchid growing myself when I get home,' she said. 'I know it's a bit late in life to start gardening but, look over there, your neighbour seems to be doing just that.' Fitzjohn followed Meg's gaze over the hedge into Rhonda Butler's garden. 'And it looks like she's going about it in a big way for a beginner, doesn't it?' That flowerbed is huge.' As she spoke, Meg came to a standstill as she surveyed its contents. 'I can't say I approve of what she's growing though.'

'Why not?' asked Fitzjohn.

'Because, unless my eyes are deceiving me, it's *pot*!'

'I assure you, Rhonda Butler would be the last person to cultivate marijuana,' replied Fitzjohn with a chuckle. 'She actively campaigns against its legalisation.'

'Then I suggest you take a closer look,' replied Meg.

Fitzjohn looked again. 'Good heavens,' he said, adjusting his glasses. 'If I wasn't seeing it with my own eyes, I wouldn't believe it, but I think you may be right.'

'I know I am but I wouldn't worry too much because those seedlings won't survive out there in the open; the conditions are all wrong.'

Fitzjohn turned to his sister. 'Since when do you know so much about the cultivation of marijuana,' he asked before a long-forgotten image came to mind of a young Meg espousing new found freedoms in 1960s London. Probably not the best time to mention her misspent youth, he thought, especially when she's showing signs of making an effort not to run everyone's life.

'I probably read about it somewhere along the line,'

replied Meg. 'The plants need high humidity and plenty of light. Another cold evening like the last one and those seedlings will shrivel.'

'Even so, now I'm aware of what she's doing, I can't ignore it.'

'What are you going to do? Send in the drug squad?' asked Meg with a snicker.

'I doubt that'll be necessary. She's probably not even aware of what she's growing. I'll go and speak to her. And it's probably best to do so now while she's out there tending her prohibited crop.' Fitzjohn left by the side gate and made his way next door.

'Good morning, Mrs Butler.'

Rhonda swung around, the spray from the hose pipe barely missing Fitzjohn's shoes. 'What do you want?' she said with a scowl.

'I'm here in my capacity as a police officer, Mrs Butler. I want to speak to you about your new garden bed.'

'My garden bed is none of your business, Mr Fitzjohn.'

'As I said, I'm here in my capacity as a police officer, so it's Detective Chief Inspector Fitzjohn, and as such, your garden bed is my business, at least concerning your choice of plants. Have you any idea what species of plant you're growing, Mrs Butler?'

'I don't need to know. My nephew has entrusted these seedling to me. He's doing a horticultural class at school and this is part of his project.' With an expression of pride, Rhonda looked over the bed. 'He lives with his parents in an apartment tower so he's not able to grow his plants at home.'

'It's admirable of you to help him.' replied Fitzjohn, eyeing the garden, 'but there's a problem. You see, what you're helping your nephew to grow is marijuana.'

'*What*? That's ridiculous. These seedling were supplied by the school specifically for the project and I don't appreciate your assumption that my nephew is into cultivating drugs,' Rhonda screeched.

'He may be as unaware as you seem to be,' said Fitzjohn. 'Nevertheless, school project or not, my advice to you is to destroy the plants and start again with something that isn't illegal, such as sun flowers or geraniums perhaps. And please do so immediately.'

'How did she take it?' asked Meg as she hovered at the kitchen window.

'Not well but that's no surprise.' Fitzjohn recounted his conversation with Rhonda. 'I doubt she knows what she's growing although I have my suspicions that her nephew does. In other words, she's been hoodwinked.'

'What are you going to do about it?'

'At this stage there's only one thing I can do. Hope she heeds what I've told her and pray to god I see geraniums growing next time I look.'

'I think you'll be disappointed because she's still watering them,' said Meg, turning back from the window. 'What about the nephew?'

'Well, I can't stand by and do nothing so a visit to his school to find out what sort of horticultural project he's involved in might be a start. I'll put Betts on it.'

CHAPTER 9

The following morning, Constance unlocked the bookshop's glass door and, followed by Harriet, stepped into an atmosphere permeated with the pleasant aromatic smell of leather and old books. 'I think I'll enjoy being here even under the circumstances,' said Harriet her eyes sparkling as she looked at row upon row of shelves, brimming with books of every description. 'Where do you want me to start?' Constance picked up a fluffy purple duster and handed it to Harriet. 'Not dusting, surely,' said Harriet with a grimace. 'I can do that at home. I was hoping for something more interesting like cataloguing or reordering the fiction section perhaps.'

'There's time for that later,' replied Constance 'It may seem trivial, but dusting is one of the most important tasks in an old building such as this. You can't expect customers to return if they choke to death while looking for a book, can you? So, get started and after I've turned on the computer system and taken delivery of this morning's supplies which should be arriving shortly, I'll make us both a cup of coffee.'

As soon as Constance disappeared into the rear of the book-shop, Harriet pranced along the rows of shelving, the duster resting every few moments on her shoulder as her attention was taken by a growing number of titles. That was until she reached "Romance". 'Oh, I've always wanted to read this,' she muttered to herself as she took the book from the shelf. As she did so, the bell on the front door tinkled. Harriet glanced over her shoulder to see two women walk in. 'Good morning. Happy to browse are we?' she asked. With nods from each, her eyes reverted to the book in her grasp whereby she barely noticed the man and another woman who entered a short-time later.

'Harriet! Still dusting are you?'

Engrossed as she was the book and the duster tumbled to the floor with a clatter at the sound of Constance's voice. 'Just finishing up,' replied Harriet, grabbing the book and shoving it into a shelf before picking up the duster and saun-tering into Constance's view.

'Thank you, I really appreciate it,' said Constance, placing two steaming cups on the counter. 'I made tea instead of coffee. I hope you don't mind.'

'No, not at all,' replied Harriet, feeling a tinge of guilt as she placed the purple duster under the counter.

'Any customers while I've been out the back?' asked Constance, her question ending with a sneeze.

'A few browsers but no sales, I'm afraid. And it's probably just as well since I'm not that confident on how to operate the till.' Constance sneezed again. 'You must be coming down with a cold.'

'It's not a cold. It's that fragrance in the air.'

Harriet took a few short sniffs. 'It's the scent of roses. Strange I didn't notice it before because it's ever so strong, isn't it? But where is it coming from?'

Constance did not reply but looked past Harriet towards the front window ledge. 'What's that over there?'

'It looks like some sort of atomizer,' replied Harriet.

Curious, Constance walked over and bent down to take a whiff of the small container. 'Well, this is definitely where that odour is coming from,' she said straightening up.

'Which means one of this morning's customers must have been the killer,' said Harriet. 'Oh, Constance. First the roses in your garden cut to ribbons and now this.'

'It seems to be the pattern.'

'What do you mean, pattern?' asked Harriet.

'The killer's,' replied Constance. 'I read in the morning newspaper that long-stemmed red roses were found thrown over poor Howard's body.'

Harriet's face drained of colour and her eyes grew round as she stared at Constance. 'We're dealing with a psychopath, aren't we? I think you should call that detective you spoke to last night and tell him what's happened.'

'I hate to make a fuss and bring him on a wild goose chase if that's what it turns out to be,' said Constance.

'It's no wild goose chase, believe me,' said Harriet as she lurched across the floor to latch the front door before flipping the sign to Closed. 'It's best that no one other than the police enter the building. It could compromise the evidence,' she said, turning back with a satisfied look.

'You've been watching too many detective shows,' said Constance, taking her mobile phone from her handbag and punching in the police detective's number.

CHAPTER 10

*F*eeling somewhat petulant from lack of sleep and the fiasco concerning Rhonda Butler's garden, Fitzjohn arrived at the station eager to find out his young sergeant's thoughts on the manuscript. On reaching the main office, however, his expectation was abruptly thwarted when he found Betts hunched over reading the text. As he approached, Betts looked up with a sheepish expression. 'I take it you didn't read the manuscript last night.'

'I decided my brain is sharper by day, sir, so I came in early this morning. I'm almost finished.'

'Well, when you are, come to my office,' replied Fitzjohn with a brusque air. 'I want to know your thoughts and to discuss something else unrelated to the case.' Somewhat miffed that while Betts slept, he had sat up half the night, Fitzjohn marched off in the direction of his office.

Half an hour later, a quiet knock on his office door drew his attention to Betts standing in the doorway, the manuscript under one arm and a mug of coffee in each hand.

'I thought coffee might help start your day off right, sir.'

'If you're suggesting my day didn't get off to a good start you'd be right,' replied Fitzjohn, sitting back in his chair. 'Come in and take a seat.' Betts handed Fitzjohn the coffee and settled himself into a chair.

'To be honest, sir, I didn't find anything that I think can help us with our investigation,' said Betts as he took the manuscript from under his arm. 'Even though all our persons of interest are mentioned, there's no reference to suggest any one of them murdered Marsha Greenwood. I think it's as Ms Parsons said, the victim planned to reveal his wife's killer in the last chapter.'

'My sentiments exactly,' replied Fitzjohn before taking a sip of the steaming brew. 'But didn't Ms Parsons also say she was to meet with the victim today to discuss that chapter?'

'I believe she did, sir.'

'Well, since that's the case, even though she told us his instructions were verbal, we can't dismiss the fact that he may have made notes in preparation for that meeting. We didn't find anything at the theatre but, considering the subject matter, I doubt he'd leave material so important to him lying around. More likely he'd keep such information at his home in Mosman. Make an application to the magistrate for a search warrant, Betts, and have the house keys released.'

'Yes, sir. What was the other matter you wanted to discuss? Something not related to the case?'

'Ah, yes. It concerns my neighbour, Rhonda Butler.'

'I thought after the last episode with the boundary between your two properties she'd have changed and become the neighbour from heaven rather than hell.'

'I thought she had until this morning when a particular incident occurred. Unfortunately, I felt I had no other choice other than to step in.' Fitzjohn put his coffee mug down and clasped his hands. 'She's growing marijuana in her back garden.'

For a long moment, Betts stared at his boss before he said with a snicker, 'You're not serious.'

'I am and it's not a laughing matter.'

'I know, sir, it's just that it's the last thing I would have thought Rhonda Butler would be involved in. Are you sure it's marijuana?'

'Meg, your future mother-in-law I might add, assured me it is and after close inspection, I had to agree with her. I didn't ask her how she gained her botanical knowledge of that particular species of plant matter,' Fitzjohn continued with a shake of his head, 'because I have a suspicion it's something to do with her 1960s hippie, flower child, past that I neither need nor want to know about.'

'Your sister was a 1960s hippie? I can't imagine. Does Sophie know?'

'I very much doubt it,' said Fitzjohn. 'And I'll leave it up to you to decide whether you wish to enlighten her or not.' Fitzjohn clasped his hands together aware of his young sergeant's amusement. 'Shall we get back to Rhonda and her gardening because you need to know the full story?' said Fitzjohn before giving an account of his neighbourly meeting with Rhonda that morning. 'Hopefully, she takes my advice and gets rid of the seedlings.'

'What about the nephew?' asked Betts.

'That is a worry. For a start, he can't be more than fifteen or sixteen years old and, it seems, has taken a turn that could lead to serious consequences. So, I'd like you to pay a visit to his school to find out what sort of horticultural project he's involved in, if any. But regardless of the result, have a word with him and his parents about the marijuana and try to find out if he's acting alone. Depending on the result we'll go from there.'

'I'll see to it, sir, but before I do, I wanted to let you know that Leo Greenwood's background check is in.'

'Ah, that's good. Does it give us any leads?'

'It may do because the day before his brother's murder, his application for a mortgage to purchase a second restaurant was knocked back. He told the bank manager he'd seek a guarantor and reapply. It could have been the reason he and his brother were talking before the performance the other night,' Betts continued. 'The timeline fits with his appointment at the bank that morning. It's purely speculation, of course, but Howard Greenwood might have refused to stand as guarantor and that could have been what Dolores Madden sensed when she went into the dressing room that evening.'

'Well, money is certainly a subject that could trigger a row between two brothers,' said Fitzjohn, 'especially since it appears the victim was financially well off if his bank accounts are anything to go by. Hopefully, our search of his property will reveal something.' As Fitzjohn spoke, his mobile phone rang.

'Fitzjohn here.'

'Chief Inspector Fitzjohn, this is Constance Parsons. You did say I should call you on this number if needs be and something has occurred that I think you should know about.' Fitzjohn listened as Constance described an overpowering scent of roses in her bookshop so strong it had all but eliminated the aroma of leather and old books. 'I do hope you don't think I'm overreacting, Chief Inspector, but I did read in the newspaper this morning that roses play a part in Howard's death, god rest his soul.'

'They do, Ms Parsons, and you've done the right thing in contacting me. Are you alone?'

'No, my friend Harriet is here with me.'

'Good. That being the case, I want you to close the bookshop for the day and both remain where you are. I'll be with you shortly.'

'That was Constance Parsons,' said Fitzjohn, turning to Betts as he hung up. 'There's been an incident at her bookshop. Once you've made that application to the magistrate for the search of Greenwood's property, we'll be on our way. I'll fill you in as we go.'

Constance Parsons could be seen opening the door of the bookshop as the two officers emerged from their car and crossed the street, dodging the traffic as they approached.

'Thank you for being so prompt, Chief Inspector,' she said as Fitzjohn and Betts stepped inside. 'I only hope I haven't brought you on a fool's errand.'

'There's no such thing where a murder investigation is concerned, Ms Parson, so I'm thankful you did call,' replied Fitzjohn. 'And I see what you mean,' he continued, sniffing the air. 'It's very heavy and definitely the scent of roses.'

'I'm glad you agree,' said Constance as their gaze fell upon the atomizer on the window ledge. Fitzjohn took off glasses and peered at it closely.

'We haven't touched it. Just in case there are fingerprints

that can be lifted,' said Harriet, looking pleased with her comment.

'That's commendable, Ms...'

'Findlay. But you can call me Harriet.'

Fitzjohn gave a quick smile before turning to Betts. 'Arrange for a forensics team, Betts.'

'Yes, sir.'

'Now, ladies,' he continued guiding the two women deeper into the bookshop, 'can you describe the customers that have come into the bookshop this morning?'

Constance looked to her friend. 'Since Harriet was the only one in the shop at the time, I think she'll be more help with that, Chief Inspector, won't you Harriet?'

'Oh, yes. Constance was out the back receiving deliveries. I was here, dusting,' said Harriet.

'And how many customers did you have during that time?' asked Fitzjohn.

'Ah, let's see. The first to arrive were two women. They were together. After that a man came in and another woman a few minutes later.'

'Can you describe the man and woman who came in alone?' asked Fitzjohn.

'I only saw them at a glance when they passed by the end of the fiction shelving so I can't give you much detail, I'm afraid, but I do remember the man was tall, fairly slim and had dark hair. I can't guess at his age because without my glasses on his face wasn't clear to me.'

'And the woman?' asked Fitzjohn.

'I saw even less of her, but I do remember she was wearing a charcoal coloured winter coat. She looked to be in her thirties, I'd say, with a fair complexion.' Harriet paused. 'I'm afraid that's all I remember, Chief Inspector.'

'Do you have CCTV in the shop, Ms Parsons?' asked Fitzjohn as he cast a speculative glance for any such security device.

'Unfortunately not, Chief Inspector.'

'Not to worry, we have Ms Finlay's descriptions which help.'

'What will happen now, Chief Inspector,' asked Constance.

'A team of scene of crime officers will arrive shortly and conduct a thorough sweep of the area for evidence. We'll work in tandem with the team and piece together and pursue any leads that may come to our attention. I'll speak to you further about the situation in the next day or so but as things stand now it would be wise to keep the bookshop closed until we've apprehended whomever left the bottle of scent.'

'Can you be reached at home, Ms Parsons, or are you staying elsewhere?'

Constance Parsons looked at Harriet who smiled. 'You can reach me at Harriet's, Chief Inspector.'

'I didn't want to worry Ms Parsons further but her situation isn't good,' said Fitzjohn as the two officers emerged from the bookshop and crossed the road to their car. 'I only hope we get a breakthrough in the case soon.'

Propelled by a strong wind, dry leaves swirled across the street to be captured in the picket fence that bordered

Howard Greenwood's garden. Fitzjohn pulled up the collar of his overcoat and together he and Betts made their way through the garden to the front door. Betts placed the key in the lock but as he did the door flew open to reveal a heavy-set woman in her mid-fifties carrying a dust-pan and brush.

'You're too early. Mr Greenwood hasn't arrived yet,' she said, eyeing the two officers warily. 'You are from the real estate, aren't you?' she added, her voice quavering.

'No, madam. We're police officers,' replied Fitzjohn, holding up his warrant card before introducing himself and Betts. 'We're investigating the death of Howard Greenwood and we have a warrant to search these premises for anything that might aid our investigation.' Fitzjohn paused, sensing the woman's unease. 'Are you a relative of Mr Greenwood?'

'No. I'm Lyn Evans, his housekeeper. I'm here to collect my things and to make sure everything is tidy before the real estate people do their valuation, although I don't think that'll be possible now. Someone must have broken in during the night because Howard's study is a shambles,' she added visibly distressed.

'Is the study the only room that's been disturbed, Mrs Evans?' Fitzjohn asked as he and Betts stepped inside and followed her through the house.

'As far as I can tell it is although I have a feeling some-one's been in Howard's bedroom as well because some of the things on the dresser aren't in their usual place.'

'We'll look at the study first if we may,' said Fitzjohn.

'It's along here,' replied the woman as she turned down a hall and abruptly stopped in an open doorway.

When they joined her, the scale of the break-in became evident as Fitzjohn's gaze took in the scene.

'Howard would be so upset to see his study in this state,'

said Mrs Evans, taking a tissue to stem the tears brimming her eyelashes. 'He was such a meticulous person and so proud of his photographic collection. It was a visual display of his years in the theatre. It's a terrible shame, it really is.'

Fitzjohn carefully entered the ransacked room the desk's drawers removed and upturned, their contents strewn over the floor along with a number of twisted metal picture frames enmeshed with their photographs ripped into shreds. Glass crunched underfoot as he approached the sole surviving frame, undisturbed on the far wall, a snapshot of the Adelphi Theatre's interior during a performance with Howard and a woman on centre stage.

'That was taken on opening night,' said Mrs Evans. 'The woman in the photograph is his wife, Marsha. She died not long after.' Mrs Evans sniffed back a tear.

'So we understand,' replied Fitzjohn. 'We were advised she died in tragic circumstances here in the house.'

'That's right. She fell down the stairs into the living room. I don't think Howard ever recovered. And now, of course, he's gone as well. It begs belief. It really does.' Lyn Evans gave a long sigh. Sensing her growing disquiet, Fitzjohn picked his way back to where she had remained in the doorway and placed a reassuring hand on her shoulder. 'I am thankful you're here, Chief Inspector because I doubt I could face Leo alone when he arrives,' she continued, fixated on the devastation. 'He's hell-bent on getting the place on the market today and with Howard not cold in his grave. It's heartless, it really is.'

'Why don't we get a breath of fresh air?' said Fitzjohn. Nodding in agreement, Lyn Evans allowed herself to be guided from the room. 'How long did you work for Howard Greenwood?' he asked as they walked through to the main part of the house and sat down near the open patio doors.

'I've been here for the past seven years, Chief Inspector. It was Marsha who employed me originally. After her death, Howard asked me to stay on. The sight of those stairs still sends a chill through me,' she said, glancing towards the sweeping glass staircase on the other side of the living room.

'Were you here the night it happened?' asked Fitzjohn.

'No. I only work through the day. Nine o'clock till three in the afternoon.'

'I see. You mentioned earlier that you're here today to collect your things and make sure everything is ready for a real estate valuation.'

'Those are my instructions from Leo. He's a callous individual but I didn't think even he would do such a thing.'

'How would you say Howard and Leo got along?' asked Fitzjohn.

'You know, I never heard Howard say anything against his brother even though I'm sure he was aware he's a wastrel. You see, Leo only came here when he wanted Howard to fund another one of his business enterprises or needed money to pay a debt. I always knew when he'd been here because Howard wasn't himself for days afterwards... as if he regretted giving in to his brother's demands yet again. It's called emotional blackmail as I'm sure you're aware, Chief Inspector. It makes me wonder if...'

'If what?' asked Fitzjohn.

'If Howard finally did refuse and paid for it with his life.' Lyn Evans stared at Fitzjohn. 'Do you think that's possible?'

'It will be considered along with other scenarios during the course of our investigation,' replied Fitzjohn, 'one of those being the memoir we understand Howard was writing with the help of a ghost writer. Do you know about that, Mrs Evans?'

'Yes, I do. Howard told me about it.'

'Do you know whether he kept any paperwork on the manuscript here at home?'

'If he did I never saw any when I was cleaning his study. As I said, Howard was meticulous. He never left anything lying around.' As Lyn Evans spoke the front door banged and a man's voice called out her name and she stiffened. 'Oh, my heavens it's Leo.'

'Don't concern yourself, Mrs Evans,' said Fitzjohn, sensing the woman's apprehension at facing Greenwood. 'I'll deal with him.'

'In that case, if you don't need me anymore, Chief Inspector, I'll leave by the back door.'

'Just one more thing before you go,' said Fitzjohn. 'Do you happen to know the name of Howard's lawyer?'

'Yes, it's Duncan Blackburn. I know because he's telephoned on occasions when Howard hasn't been at home. I think he has an office in the city, but I can't tell you where.'

'That's not a problem. The name is enough. Thank you, Mrs Evans.'

Just after Lyn Evans had grabbed her handbag along with a small cardboard box containing her personal items and left, Leo Greenwood burst into the living room. 'What the hell are you doing here,' he yelled, glaring at Fitzjohn, 'and where's the housekeeper?'

'And good morning to you too, Mr Greenwood,' said Fitzjohn. 'Mrs Evans, the housekeeper, has done as you requested. She hasn't lingered unnecessarily and as for myself, I have a warrant to search the property,' Fitzjohn handed the document to Greenwood.

'For what?' asked Greenwood, scanning the warrant.

'As it says, paperwork pertaining to your brother's manuscript and any information we might gather to assist us in our investigation into his death. I take it you are aware he was writing his memoir?'

'He mentioned it but I can't see what it has to do with your investigation, so I'd appreciate it if you'd leave. I'm expecting a team of real estate agents to value the property at any moment and your presence is not required.' As he spoke, several SOCOs could be seen being ushered towards the study by Betts. 'Good god. Who are they?' Leo barked, throwing his hands in the air.

'They're scene of crime officers,' Fitzjohn replied. 'They've been called in because there's been a break-in during the night. Consequently, I have to inform you that neither the valuation nor the sale of the property will be possible at this time since it's now part of our investigation into your brother's death. In other words, the property is inaccessible to you or the real estate. You'll be notified as soon as the restriction has been lifted.'

'But...'

'I'll show you out,' said Fitzjohn as he ushered Greenwood from the living room and along the hallway to the front door.

Fitzjohn returned to the study where Betts hovered in the doorway, watching the SOCOs at work. 'Has anything been found?' he asked.

'Only that it appears as though the back of the one remaining photograph on the wall was cut open and possibly searched before being hung back up, sir. Seems to be a strange thing to do since all the rest have been smashed to pieces and the photographs torn up.'

'Perhaps the frame held what the intruder was looking for but as you say, why hang it up again?' Fitzjohn thought for a moment. 'I wonder if it had something to do with the subject matter. Mrs Evans said it's a photograph of the play's opening night before Marsha Greenwood's death. Bag it up, Betts. We'll take it with us. Anything else?'

'Only that it looks like the intruder came and went via those french doors,' replied Betts, gesturing across the room to where several panes of glass could be seen missing around the door handle. 'Was that Leo Greenwood I heard you talking to?' he continued, changing the subject.

'Yes.' Fitzjohn recounted their conversation. 'After speaking to Mrs Evans, I doubt there was much love lost between he and his brother especially if you take into account his arrangement this morning for the valuation of his home at such an early stage.'

'In which case, he must be fairly certain he's the sole beneficiary,' said Betts.

'One would think so if in fact our victim left a will. We'll speak to his lawyer. Mrs Evans gave me his name. Duncan Blackburn. Find out where he can be reached, Betts.'

'Yes, sir.'

'I've located Duncan Blackburn, sir,' said Betts as he secured Howard Greenwood's home before he followed Fitzjohn through the garden to the car. 'He has offices on York Street in the city. Blackburn & O'Dea, Lawyers. They deal specifically with wills, probate and estates.'

'Good, we'll make our way there now.'

~

The two officers entered Duncan Blackburn's office to the sound of raised voices. 'Can I help you?' asked a young woman who sat behind the reception desk, her voice shrill in an effort, Fitzjohn thought, to mask the commotion from behind a closed door.

'We're from the police,' he replied, raising his own voice a decibel as he showed his warrant card. 'DCI Fitzjohn and DS Betts. We wish to speak to Mr Blackburn in regard to one of his clients.'

'As you can, no doubt, hear, he's with clients, Chief Inspector, and I have no idea how long he'll be,' replied the woman, flinching with each additional bellow from within.

'Do you think he'll come out alive?' asked Fitzjohn.

'Being an estate lawyer has its drawbacks but he's survived so far.'

As she spoke the door to Blackburn's office flew open to reveal a middle-aged couple followed by a woman in her forties. A short, stout, man with a shock of dark hair and a rumpled grey suit followed shortly thereafter. 'Good day to you Mr and Mrs Perkins, Mrs Braithwaite,' he called after them, his voice trailing off as the three walked out of the office. As they did so, he became aware of Fitzjohn and Betts.

'These gentlemen are from the police, Mr Blackburn,' said the receptionist.

'Ah! If I'd known you were here, I'd have had you arrest that trio,' he said with a chuckle. 'Duncan Blackburn,' he announced, straightening his suit coat before he adjusted his dark rimmed glasses. 'How can I help you?'

'We're investigating the death of a man by the name of Howard Greenwood,' replied Fitzjohn. 'We understand he's one of your clients.'

'He is indeed,' Chief Inspector. I was saddened to read about the unfortunate circumstances of his death in the newspaper. It makes one wonder what's wrong with society when a decent man is slain. Come through to my office, gentlemen and hopefully I can assist you.' Fitzjohn and Betts followed Blackburn into his office. 'Please, make yourselves comfortable,' he continued gesturing to the chairs in front of his desk while he picked up an overturned chair. 'Unfortunately, some of my clients become overwrought when they realise they haven't been remembered in their loved one's last will and testament.'

'Does it happen often?' asked Fitzjohn as Blackburn sat down at his desk with a sigh.

'Unfortunately, where money is concerned the hackles come out in, not all, but certainly in some people. Often in those you least expect so it comes as a bit of a shock,' replied Blackburn. 'One of the drawbacks to being an estate lawyer,' he added as he gathered a number of papers on his desk together and placed them in the "Out" tray. 'Now, concerning Howard Greenwood. I assume you're here to find out who his beneficiaries are. It's usually the reason when I get a visit from the police.'

'It is, as a matter of fact,' replied Fitzjohn. 'The beneficiaries are one of the factors we have to consider during our investigation even though it may not have anything to do with the victim's demise.'

'Indeed, and with that in mind, I had his will released

from our safe custody facility. I have it here,' he continued, taking a file from a different tray.

'How long has Mr Greenwood been your client,' asked Fitzjohn.

'For many years although we only met when he wished to make changes to his will, the last of which was shortly after the death of his wife, Marsha Greenwood. She had been his sole beneficiary and would have inherited the entire estate had she lived.'

'And now?' asked Fitzjohn.

'There's still only one beneficiary,' said Blackburn, opening the file in front of him, 'The Chalmaris School of Acting of which Howard was a founding member and in which he has been actively involved for the past twenty-three years. The school will receive all monies, debenture stocks, as well as Howard's home in Mosman. And I must say, he's been extremely thorough in his instructions as to how the house is to be used. It's to become accommodation for interstate and overseas students of the school. If that is not found to be possible due to zoning regulations, the property is to be sold with all proceeds going to buy a property where accommodation for the students is possible.'

'Did he give a reason for not including his brother as a beneficiary?' asked Fitzjohn.

'He did as a matter of fact. He said he felt that after years of bestowing upon him many thousands of dollars, all of which he squandered on misguided business practices, and having no offspring, he wanted his estate to be used for a worthwhile purpose that was close to his heart. Nevertheless, I advised my client that if he failed to include his brother, there was every likelihood he would contest the will. And since he chose not to heed my warning, well, you can call me a cynic if you like, Chief Inspector, but I see a legal battle ahead in which case my client's last wishes won't be realised for some time, if at all. There is, of course, one certainty. The legal profession will benefit.'

'After this morning's incident with Leo Greenwood concerning the sale of his brother's house, it's going to come as a shock when he finds out he isn't mentioned in the will.' said Fitzjohn as the two officers made their way down in the elevator. 'I think Mr Blackburn is right in expecting a long, drawn out, legal battle because I can't see Leo giving up without a fight.'

'It doesn't seem like Leo is alone if that incident in Blackburn's office is anything to go by,' said Betts. 'I know money can be a strong motive for murder but for some reason it never occurred to me that an estate lawyer had to deal with such irate clients. No wonder the man's cynical.' At that moment Betts' mobile phone rang and after a brief conversation, he turned to Fitzjohn. 'That was Williams calling from the Adelphi Theatre, sir. He believes they've found the murder weapon. A rolled-up newspaper wrapped in cling plastic. It was found in a garbage disposal unit in the laneway outside the theatre. It's being taken to forensics as we speak.'

'A tightly rolled up newspaper can be a devastating weapon?' said Fitzjohn as they returned to the car. 'And it fits Charles Conroy's description. A soft object that left microscopic pieces of plastic on the victim's skin. Let's hope it is the murder weapon and leads us to our killer.'

As the sky darkened in the early evening, Betts pulled into the parking area at the rear of the station and the two officers made their way into the building. 'We'll speak to Williams as soon as he returns and then we'll call it a day,' said Fitzjohn. 'Meg told me this morning that she's invited you and Sophie for dinner, and I promised I wouldn't keep you late. And a word of warning, she also made it clear neither of us are to talk shop.'

'That'll be difficult with everything that's happened in the past couple of days,' said Betts. 'But don't worry, you can leave it to me. I'll buy her flowers on my way over.'

'Ah! So, you think you can charm my sister, do you?' Fitzjohn chuckled. 'Believe me, it won't work. I know because over the years, I've tried.'

'It takes a certain kind of knack, sir.'

Fitzjohn opened the front door and breathed in the aroma of food and heard the sound of female voices as he stepped inside. Obviously, Sophie had already arrived, and Meg appeared to be maintaining the positive change in her manner if their laughter was anything to go by, he thought as he placed his briefcase on the hall table. Of course, Betts will think it's the result of his charismatic personality but, perhaps that would not be such a bad thing since marrying Sophie means he has many years of Meg to look forward to. So, a positive start to that journey would be best. With a snicker, he started along the hallway towards the kitchen.

'Hello, ladies, I'm home,' he called. Reaching the doorway, he found the room empty. 'Hello?'

'We're in the conservatory,' came Meg's whispered voice.

'In the dark?' asked Fitzjohn, pushing the half-closed door open.

'We're observing the goings on next door, Uncle Alistair,' said Sophie, giving Fitzjohn a peck on the cheek. 'We didn't turn on the light because we don't want to appear nosey.'

'But you are being nosey,' said Fitzjohn, straining his neck and adjusting his glasses as he peered through the window and over the hedge into Rhonda's back garden.

'Nonsense. We're merely concerned neighbours wishing to uphold the good standard of the neighbourhood,' replied Meg. 'But unfortunately, the way things are going it looks like it's all downhill from here. And to think that earlier today, I thought Mrs Butler had taken your advice and got rid of the cannabis seedlings because I did see her planting flowers in that garden bed. But that hope drained away when the workmen arrived and started erecting the greenhouse.'

'Greenhouse!'

'I'm afraid so. It's obvious she's decided to expand her operation.' Meg squinted into the darkness. 'You don't happen to have night vision glasses do you Alistair?'

'No. It's not something I have use for,' replied Fitzjohn surprised at his sister's unusual request.

'Oh, that's too bad because I doubt we'll be able to see much else this evening. I wanted to see whether they're adding lighting. That would really accelerate the growing process and no doubt ensure the seedlings survival ten-fold.'

'Mum? I didn't realise you knew so much about the culti-vation of marijuana.' Sophie turned to Fitzjohn with a ques-tioning look.

Wishing to divert Sophie's attention from the mystery of her mother's apparent horticultural knowledge that had the potential to ruin Meg's new-found favourable manner,

Fitzjohn said, 'I'll have another word with Rhonda in the morning before I leave for the station and see if I can find out just what's going on.'

'Good evening, everyone.' The three turned to see Betts' silhouette in the doorway, a spray of flowers in each hand. 'Why are you in the dark?' Fitzjohn turned on the lamp in the corner of the conservatory. 'Flowers for the ladies,' Betts continued, handing a spray to Sophie with a peck on her cheek before giving a spray to Meg with a wide smile and a slight bow.

'Oh, how thoughtful of you, Martin,' said Meg. 'You're so sweet. Thank you very much. I can't remember when I last received flowers. Aren't you a lucky girl to have such a wonderful fiancé, Sophie?' she continued as the two women bustled away to put the flowers in water.

'That got you off on the right footing,' said Fitzjohn.

Betts raised his eyebrows and grinned. 'It's not difficult when you know how, sir.' Fitzjohn did not reply, happy to let Betts bask in his glory. 'You didn't say why you were here in the dark.'

'Take a look out of the window into Mrs Butler's garden.'

'It's a bit dark to see very much but it looks like a green-house under construction.'

'That's exactly what it is,' replied Fitzjohn. 'I daresay the workmen will return tomorrow to complete the job. There's no law against it, of course, but from Meg's observations during the day, I suspect Rhonda plans to move the cannabis seedlings inside.'

'Martin, darling. Alistair. Come along,' came Meg's voice from the kitchen. 'We're about to start serving dinner.'

'If you gave her flowers she might call you darling as well,' said Betts with a smirk.

The following morning and after seeing the marijuana seedlings still sprouting in amongst the newly planted flowers, Fitzjohn felt duty-bound to call on Rhonda Butler yet again. He entered her garden just as she emerged from the house wearing a pink dressing gown and a pair of fluffy green slippers.

'What are you doing here?' she snapped.

'Good morning, Mrs Butler. I'm sure you're well aware of the reason I'm here. It's because you've chosen to ignore my warning about the seedlings.'

'I've told you before, my seedlings are none of your business.'

'As a police officer, they are my business.' Fitzjohn paused as his exasperation grew. 'Look, Mrs Butler, I know we've had our problems in the past but nevertheless, I don't want to see you get into trouble over this issue. Growing an illicit substance is a serious matter.'

Rhonda gave Fitzjohn a scornful look. 'Get off my property.'

'Very well,' replied Fitzjohn, 'but first I have to advise that if you choose not to heed my warning I'll have to take the matter further which will mean you'll face the full force of the law. Good day.'

CHAPTER 11

*W*ith his morning newspaper tucked under his arm, Fitzjohn emerged from the taxi and made his way into the station. After he acknowledged the constable on duty at the front desk, he released the security door and stepped into the main office area. Immediately, his attention was taken by a tall, heavy-set, man leaving Peta Ashby's office. Fitzjohn slowed his pace and observed the figure retreat towards the station's rear entrance. 'Grieg,' he whispered under his breath. As he uttered the name, Peta emerged into the hallway and their eyes met.

'Can I have a word, Fitzjohn?' she asked.

'Yes, ma'am.' Fitzjohn followed the chief superintendent into her office.

'I've just had a visitor. Inspector Grieg,' she said, sitting down at her desk.

'So I noticed. Did he say what's brought him back to Sydney?' Fitzjohn asked, settling himself into a chair.

'A death in the family, by all accounts. An uncle, I believe. He's been given compassionate leave to attend the funeral.

He says he called into the station to see a few of the old faces.'

'Well, he's not without supporters who were willing to do his bidding for favours while he was here as the chief super-intendent?'

'I don't doubt it. People like Grieg usually do. What worries me, Fitzjohn, is that he might be pulling in some of those favours to make your life difficult. I noticed he spent quite a long time in the incident room with Constable Smithers.'

'Ah, yes. Smithers was one of Grieg's more active minions, for want of a better word. Maybe he still is.'

'Well, I wouldn't know about that, but I did get the feeling something is afoot because they were tucked away in there for some time.' Peta thought for a moment. 'Is Smithers part of your investigative team into the Greenwood case?'

'Yes. Betts has him working on the background checks.' Which, come to think of it, is taking an unusually long time to materialise, Fitzjohn thought to himself. Perhaps Smithers is already in the process of sabotaging the operation.

'Well, whatever he's working on, I advise you to watch your back,' said Peta.

'I will.' Fitzjohn got to his feet but as he did so, he hesitated.

'Is there something else?' asked Peta.

'Yes, there is…' Fitzjohn hesitated and fought back the overwhelming urge to tell Peta how he felt about her. 'There's been somewhat of a breakthrough in the case,' he said at last. 'We believe we may have found the murder weapon. I'll keep you posted.'

A sense of frustration seared through him as he left Peta and carried on through the station to his office. Why didn't I just tell her? he asked himself as he opened the door and stepped inside. Because it would compromise what I believe in as far as the smooth running of the station goes and lead to problems in the end, he argued. With a sigh he placed his newspaper and briefcase on the desk and shrugged out of his suit coat before sitting down heavily into his chair. As he did so, Grieg's reappearance came to mind. Why am I surprised he's back? After all, he sees me as being responsible for not only his demotion but also his fall from grace and banishment to the farthest reaches of the state. He won't be satisfied until he has his revenge. As this thought materialised, Betts appeared in the doorway carrying two folders.

'Ah, morning, Betts. Any news?'

'Yes, sir. I have Dolores Madden and Simon Roach's background checks,' Betts replied, handing Fitzjohn two folders.

'And not before time,' replied Fitzjohn, his eyebrows knitting together as he opened each folder out on his desk in front of him. As he did, Smithers came to mind. 'Things aren't moving quick enough, Betts. At this stage we should have far more information on everyone concerned with that theatre. We're still waiting on Stephanie Mowbray's, aren't we? See what you can do to hurry things up.'

'I will, sir.' Betts pulled out a chair and sat down. 'Madden's background check offers a few interesting insights, one being that our victim tried on more than one occasion to have her dismissed. The most recent attempt was still undetermined when the theatre closed. On all previous occasions, she threatened to take the theatre's management to court for unfair dismissal.'

'Hence, we can assume there was no love lost between

Dolores and Howard Greenwood,' said Fitzjohn, his keen eyes scanning the contents of the folder. 'The question is, would she kill him in order to save her job?'

'Considering she's in her late fifties, it could be difficult for her to get another such position without a good reference,' said Betts. 'I looked into her financial affairs and she wouldn't have managed without being employed. She has no savings.'

'In which case, being dismissed could have had dire consequences for her,' said Fitzjohn. 'And not only that. While reading the manuscript, I got the distinct feeling that not only did Howard not get along with Madden but his wife, Marsha, didn't either.'

Fitzjohn looked down at the second folder.

'As far as Roach goes, as you'll note, his background check does offer one unexpected insight,' said Betts. 'It concerns plagiarism. As we already know, Howard was not only an actor but also a playwright and it seems that recently, Roach accused him of plagiarising one of his written works. In fact, he threatened to take legal action on the matter. Howard Greenwood made it clear to Roach that if he went ahead, he'd make sure that none of his plays would ever see another performance. In other words, he'd ruin his career as a playwright. Even so, the two kept up appearances and Roach was invited to the party.'

'I guess as the person who wrote that particular play, it was expected on its closing night,' replied Fitzjohn. 'Anything else I should know?'

'Only that it's rumoured Roach and Marsha Greenwood had an affair but whether that's true or not...'

'Mmm. Rumours aren't facts which are what we work with,' said Fitzjohn. 'However, we do know that Simon

Roach had the means, opportunity and motive to kill Howard Greenwood as did Howard's brother Leo, so we're not lacking in persons of interest, are we? Even so, is there anyone else we should add to that list?' asked Fitzjohn, his eyes scanning the directory of actors and employees of the theatre.

'We haven't spoken to Madelaine Wells yet, sir. She's the woman who took over Marsha Greenwood's role in the play.'

'Ah, yes, she became ill during the closing night's performance and left immediately after the play finished so didn't attend the celebrations,' said Fitzjohn, sitting back in his chair. 'And yet Simon Roach believes he saw her in the laneway when he left the theatre. He may have been mistaken, of course, but we'll speak to her next.' Fitzjohn closed both folders. 'Before we do, however, how is the other matter concerning Rhonda Butler coming along?'

'I have an appointment with the headmaster of her nephew's school this afternoon, sir.'

'Ah, good because with that greenhouse going up and since speaking to Rhonda again this morning, I have a feeling there's no time to lose. She isn't cooperating nor, I suspect, does she intend to. The whole matter needs to be dealt with, and quickly. I feel it in my bones. In the meantime, however, let's speak to Madelaine Wells.'

Betts turned off the hustle and bustle of Marion Street in Leichhardt, with its restaurants and cafes, onto a quiet tree-lined avenue before pulling up in front of a Victorian terrace house. 'Madelaine Wells rents this property, sir,' he said as the two officers climbed out of the car. Fitzjohn eyed the peeling paintwork on the front door as they reached the porch, its surface covered in dust along with dried leaves blown there by the gusting wind. As he did, the front door opened and a woman in her late thirties with shoulder-length fair hair appeared, carrying a handbag.

'Can I help you?' she asked with a look of wariness as the two officers mounted the porch steps.

'Ms Wells?' asked Fitzjohn.

'Yes.'

'I'm DCI Fitzjohn and this is DS Betts.' Fitzjohn held up his warrant card. 'We're investigating the death of Howard Greenwood and we understand he was a colleague of yours.'

'Yes, that's right. I played the leading female role opposite Howard in his latest play. I couldn't believe it when I heard he'd been killed. It's terrible.'

'As you worked closely with Mr Greenwood we'd just like to ask if you saw or heard anything that might help us in our investigation, no matter how insignificant it might seem.'

'Well, as you can see I'm on my way out. Can you come back later?'

'It won't take more than a few minutes,' said Fitzjohn. 'Did you?'

'No. I can't say as I did other than the fact we were all feeling somewhat low because the play was closing. It's meant steady employment for us for quite some time and you never know how long it will be before you get another part or how long it will run.'

'We understand there was a farewell party after the performance.'

'Yes. Howard organised it. But I didn't attend. I suffer from migraines. Not often but I could feel one coming on during the third act and I knew I had to come home because I can become quite ill.'

'That's unfortunate,' said Fitzjohn. 'By any chance did you speak to Howard before you left the theatre?'

'No. After the performance and the curtain calls, he went straight to his dressing room.' Madelaine paused. 'Look, you may as well know now, because I'm sure someone will tell you anyway, that Howard and I didn't exactly see eye to eye. He rarely made conversation with me.'

'Oh? Was there any particular reason?' asked Fitzjohn.

'I can only think it was resentment, Chief Inspector. You see, my role had previously been played by Howard's wife, Marsha. She died in an accident a couple of years ago.'

'So we understand. It was at a Christmas party, wasn't it?'

'It was, yes.'

'Were you there at the time?'

'Yes. The whole cast was there. It was an awful night. Things deteriorated after that; with Howard, that is. As time went along, he became increasingly difficult to work with. His grief, I suppose.' Margo paused. 'I know it's not nice to speak ill of him, especially now, but to be honest, I wasn't surprised when I heard he'd been murdered.'

'So you believe there were those who might have wished him harm?' asked Fitzjohn.

'I really couldn't say. I just know he was confrontational at the best of times and did have arguments with the cast and the crew from time to time.' Margo looked at her watch with an air of impatience.

'We won't keep you much longer, Ms Wells,' said Fitzjohn. 'Just one more question. Can you confirm what time you left the theatre?'

'It was after the last curtain call. I booked an Uber and it came almost immediately. Just after eleven. It's only a ten or fifteen minutes' drive. Here, I'll show you.' Margo rummaged in her handbag for her phone and scrolled down the screen. 'Here's my Uber booking,' she said, turning the small screen toward Fitzjohn. 'As you can see, the driver dropped me here at eleven-twenty.' Margo met Fitzjohn's gaze with a satisfied look. 'I was feeling so ill by that time, I came in and went straight to bed.'

'So you didn't return to the theatre later on?'

'Why would I do that? As I said, I wasn't well.'

'I only ask because you were seen in the laneway at approximately twelve-thirty a.m., Ms Wells,' Fitzjohn replied.

'But that's ridiculous. Whoever told you that is mistaken.'

Under a slate grey sky with the first drops of rain splattering the pavement, the two officers walked briskly to their car. 'Well, one thing seems clear,' said Fitzjohn, rubbing his hands together to generate a bit of warmth before he opened the passenger door. 'Howard Greenwood was difficult to get along with and so consequently, wasn't liked by those who knew him. What isn't clear, however, is whether Simon Roach was mistaken about seeing Madelaine Wells in the laneway that night or is she lying?'

'It's a stone's throw to the theatre from here, sir. It's possible she may have walked back.'

'My thoughts precisely,' replied Fitzjohn. 'Let's keep that in mind, shall we? After all, she could have feigned illness to provide herself with an alibi.'

Betts looked at his watch. 'I'd better get over to the school for my appointment with the headmaster, sir.'

'Seeing you're going that way, perhaps you can drop me at the theatre,' said Fitzjohn. 'I want to take another look at the crime scene and the theatre in general. Just to satisfy myself that I haven't missed anything. You can join me there later.'

∼

The stage door refused to open on his first attempt, warped as it was by the damp weather. Fitzjohn gave it a gentle shove and stepped into the dimly lit space, where dust particles filled the air causing an uncontrollable sneeze. Roused by Fitzjohn's outburst, a security guard, slight in stature, appeared in the doorway of his small office, a questioning look across his face.

'I'm sorry, sir, the theatre is no longer open to the public.'

'I'm not the public. I'm a police officer. DCI Fitzjohn.' Fitzjohn showed his warrant card as he spoke and at the same time, tried to stem another sneeze.

'I was told the police had finished here,' replied the security guard. 'As soon as the crew have done packing up their equipment, I'll be closing the building down.'

'I shan't be long. I just want to have a final look at the crime scene.'

'Well, I hope you're the last person who decides they want to take another look around the place.'

'Why, have you had others?' asked Fitzjohn.

'Mmm. The guy who wrote the play was here wanting to take photographs of the auditorium.'

'Simon Roach?'

'Yes, that's his name. Beats me why he left it till the last minute. His play's been running here for the past eighteen months.'

'No doubt he was prompted by the theatre's imminent destruction,' said Fitzjohn.

~

Where once the hurly-burly of performers scurrying towards the wings filled the maze of backstage passageways, and the sound of voices of those on the stage reverberated throughout the auditorium, Fitzjohn continued on, deeper into the building, its silence now only broken by the creak of the floorboards underfoot. When he reached Howard Greenwood's dressing room, he drew back in surprise to see Dolores Madden rummaging through the drawers of the dresser.

'Ms Madden.'

Dolores spun around, wavering as she did so. 'Chief Inspector, you startled me,' she said with a laugh. 'I was just making sure there weren't any costumes left in here.' As she spoke, Dolores slipped her hand into her jacket pocket. 'But then I wished I hadn't come in,' she added, looking down at the floor where the victim's body had lain. 'The sight of Howard just won't leave me. Anyway, I must carry on,' she continued making for the doorway. 'I still have things to pack.'

'Before you go, Ms Madden, you may be able to help answer a question that's come up. I seem to remember you saying that you didn't attend the after-performance party and yet one of those who did remembered seeing a woman dressed in an electric blue gown with gold beading. It sounds similar to the one you were wearing when we spoke yesterday.'

'Are you accusing me of lying to you, Chief Inspector?' replied Dolores with an air of indignance. 'Because, if you are, you'll be sorely disappointed, the reason being there are two such gowns. Come, I'll show you.' Dolores bustled past Fitzjohn and along the passageway to the costume department. There, hanging on a rack on the back wall were two identical gowns.

'Do you know who wore the other gown last night?' asked Fitzjohn at the same time wondering what she had slipped into her jacket pocket.

'No, I don't,' bristled Dolores. 'The gown was here when I left the theatre so I can only think that whichever cast member it was, came in here before the party and helped herself.'

Disinclined to pursue the matter further, Fitzjohn left Dolores to return to the scene of the crime where he found Betts on the threshold, looking into the room.

'Has being here helped in any way, sir?'

'No, not really,' replied Fitzjohn, 'other than the fact that Dolores Madden appears to be a petty thief. When I arrived, she was in here rifling through the victim's possessions, but it doesn't mean to say she's our killer. What was the result of your inquiries with the headmaster?'

'It's as you suspected, sir. Rhonda Butler's nephew isn't enrolled in any horticultural classes. In fact, his school doesn't run any such courses.'

'Mmm. On that account, I'll have to put Mrs Butler straight on the matter,' said Fitzjohn as he and Betts entered the crime scene.

CHAPTER 12

*C*onstance turned over the cardboard sign that hung from a hook on the bookshop glass door to Closed and reached to flick off the light switch before she stepped out into the cold night air. As she did, the telephone on the wall next to the counter rang. She hovered at the door for a moment, undecided whether or not to bother answering it. It had been a long day with an abundance of customers and deliveries, and she felt weary. But then again, perhaps I should, she thought. After all, it might be about that call I'm waiting on regarding the book fair.

'Hello,' she said, placing her keys and handbag on the counter.

'Ms Parsons, it's Detective Sergeant Betts.'

'Oh, hello, Sergeant,' replied Constance after a moment's hesitation. 'You only just caught me. I was just about to leave for the day. I hope this is to tell me you've solved the case.'

'Not yet but we do have a new lead and since it's in relation to the manuscript, Chief Inspector Fitzjohn wonders if you'd be able to meet him at the theatre.'

'You mean now?'

'Yes. He realises it's an imposition, but it could help our investigation.'

'I see. Well, I suppose I could drop by there on my way home if it's that important although, I can't see that I can add anything more to what I've already told you both.'

'It concerns not only the manuscript, Ms Parsons but Howard Greenwood's dressing room. The Chief Inspector would like your views on whether anything has changed since you were last there and since the building is about to be demolished...'

'Oh yes, of course. It's the last chance really, isn't it? All right, I'll meet you there but with the traffic as it is at this time of day, it'll probably take me a good half hour.'

With a soft rain falling, the wet pavement glistened under the street lights as Constance climbed out of the taxi in front of the theatre. When she did, she looked up at the dark edifice, its windows now boarded, the life and vitality of the building gone forever. Such a shame, she thought with a sigh as she started along the laneway, deserted but for a car parked in the shadows. Obviously the chief inspector's she told herself, buttoning her coat against the dank air. When she reached the stage door, it stood ajar. It creaked as she pushed it open and stepped inside, her senses instantly assaulted by a musty odour of damp and mould in the already dusty atmosphere.

'Chief Inspector,' she called, reluctant to walk alone any further into the gloomy interior. While she listened and waited, her thoughts turned from the silence to the electrifying atmosphere that had met her on previous occasions, brought to life by the performers festooned in their costumes, each clamouring to reach the wings. All at once, however, the mental image faded and as silence returned, she caught sight of a light now radiating in the distance through the murky dimness. It's coming from Howard's dressing room I think, she said to herself as she peered ahead. With a sense of apprehension at the thought of witnessing the scene where he had died, she tentatively moved forward towards the light.

'Chief Insp... Oh,' she uttered as she reached the doorway to Howard's dressing room and stared inside, the space empty but for the familiar trappings of his theatrical life. For a moment or two she lingered, almost as if she expected him to appear and invite her in as he usually did, but that sensation vanished when she heard footsteps. Reassured, she stepped back into the passageway expecting to catch her first glimpse of the chief inspector and his sergeant but there was no one there. In the deathly silence that followed, she remained still, reluctant to walk further into the shadows as a growing sense of unease took hold. 'I'm being ridiculous,' she muttered at last. 'What's there to be scared of? After all, it's just a dark, deserted building.' With that, she took a deep breath and walked on to the end of the hallway where she turned the corner to see another light emanating from one of the rooms. Oh, no wonder they couldn't hear me. They're in the farthest reaches,' she thought as she quickened her step, anxious to end her isolation. When she reached the room's threshold, however, a gasp left her lips and she shuddered as her eyes fell upon Dolores Madden's body lying on the floor in a pool of blood and festooned with long-stemmed red roses.

Her heart racing, Constance stood transfixed in fear,

before she staggered backwards. Stumbling in the half-light, she retraced her steps, but had she? Confused she stared into the labyrinth of choices. Which passageway led to the stage door? It was then a gurgled laugh sounded, its echo surrounding her before a silhouette of a shadowed figure approached out of the darkness.

CHAPTER 13

*W*eary from the long day, Fitzjohn and Betts drove in silence to the sound of the rain and the repetitious rhythm of the wiper blades on the windscreen. 'If you'd told me we'd be here at the theatre again tonight to attend another homicide, I wouldn't have believed you,' said Fitzjohn as Betts turned into the laneway. 'Do we know who the victim is?'

'No, sir. Also, there's a possibility that there's more than one homicide because, apparently, there was some confusion in the mind of the person who reported the crime. Consequently, the dispatcher wasn't able to be clear on the details.' Betts pulled over to the side of the laneway behind a number of other police vehicles.

'Who reported the crime?'

'The demolition team's foreman, sir.'

'Well, hopefully, he'll be able to shed light on what happened here tonight,' said Fitzjohn as they left the car and dodged the puddles, sprinting towards the stage door. After showing their warrant cards to the constable on duty, they entered the building, its atmosphere now humming with activity.

'Good evening, sir.'

'Evening, Sergeant,' replied Fitzjohn, turning to see an officer standing behind the door. 'Which way is the crime scene?'

'There are two, sir. The first straight ahead to the end of the hallway and turn right. You'll find the pathologist there attending to the body.'

'And the second?' asked Fitzjohn, his spirits plummeting.

The second is further along, sir, although the victim is being transported to St. Vincent's Hospital as we speak.'

'Thank heaven for small mercies,' mumbled Fitzjohn as he and Betts carried on, deeper into the theatre. When they reached the end of the hallway and turned to the right, Fitzjohn hesitated as his gaze was attracted to the light shining from what he knew to be the costume department. With a sense of foreboding, he moved ahead to be met with the gruesome scene of Dolores Madden's blood soaked body.

'Good evening, gentlemen,' said Charles Conroy, looking up, his face drawn with fatigue. 'We have more roses.'

'So it seems,' replied Fitzjohn as he and Betts joined Charles next to the body. 'Which might suggest we're dealing with the same killer if it weren't for the fact this woman was stabbed.'

'And not just once,' said Charles. 'I've recorded three wounds, one severing the aorta, the largest artery in the body. Let's just say she would have died quickly.'

'Can you estimate time of death?' asked Fitzjohn.

'I'd say between eight and ten o'clock this evening.'

Fitzjohn looked at Betts, his face white. 'Betts, find the

foreman who reported the crimes this evening and have a word with him, would you, please?'

'Yes, sir.'

'Other than the roses, do you see any other similarities to Howard Greenwood's killing?' he asked, turning back to Charles.

'Only that, as in the Greenwood murder, she doesn't appear to have put up a struggle,' replied Charles, looking down at the body, 'so it indicates she knew her assailant. Of course, there is the possibility that something might come to light during the post mortem that suggests otherwise. This isn't the only crime scene, however, as I'm sure you're aware. Another woman was found unconscious in the wings. She sustained a head injury and is clinging to life. I'd say it's touch and go whether she survives.'

'Fleeing from whoever did this, no doubt,' said Fitzjohn as he looked down at Dolores's body and shuddered. 'Do you have any idea who the other woman is?' he continued.

'I believe her name is Parsons.'

'Constance Parsons?' Fitzjohn winced and passed Charles an agonising look.

'Yes, that's her given name. Constance. Have you met her through your investigation into Greenwood's death?'

'Yes, her connection being that she was ghost writing his memoir. The question is, why was she here?'

Fitzjohn left Charles and retraced his steps through the maze of passageways in search of his young sergeant whom he found in a room some distance away. As he entered, Betts turned around.

'This is where the foreman found the other victim, sir. No where near the costume department so it's difficult to say whether she witnessed Dolores Madden's murder. The good news is the foreman arrived in time. She's alive.'

'So Charles said,' replied Fitzjohn. 'What I can't understand is why she was here in the theatre in the first place. The injured woman is Constance Parsons.' Betts stared at Fitzjohn. 'Charles seems to think it's touch and go as to whether she'll make it.' Fitzjohn fell silent. 'I should have done more to protect her.'

'You weren't to know she'd come here tonight, sir,' replied Betts.

'Even so, I should have made her more aware of the danger she was in and I didn't.'

'You didn't want to frighten her more than she already was, sir.'

'That's true, but there is a certain balance you need to reach between the two, and in this case, I didn't find it, Betts.' Fitzjohn looked around the dimly lit room filled with discarded chairs.

'The only explanation I can think of as to why she was found here is that she became disorientated while she ran away from whoever attacked her,' said Betts.

'It's possible,' replied Fitzjohn. 'This place is a maze at the best of times. Under those circumstances I should imagine it'd be impossible to navigate. I think we have two scenarios to look at. The first that Ms Parsons witnessed the murder and ran for her life and lost her way. The second, that the murder happened before or after she was attacked, and she saw nothing. But as I said, it puzzles me why she was here.'

'She could have been set up, sir. Maybe they both were.'

'It wouldn't surprise me,' replied Fitzjohn, 'because I

think you'll agree that when we left here earlier today, we were both under the impression that Dolores Madden, along with the rest of the crew, had left the building. And Constance Parsons certainly had no reason to come here.'

'If she doesn't survive, we may never know what really happened,' said Betts. 'She was unconscious when the foreman found her. In fact, he thought she was dead.'

'Did he find Dolores Madden also?'

'No. She was discovered by the police officers who attended the call out,'

'Let's get to the hospital and see how Ms Parsons is,' said Fitzjohn.

It was close to one a.m., when the two officers arrived at St Vincent's Hospital and emerged from the elevator into the Intensive Care Unit. Fitzjohn approached the nurses' station where a man in his mid-fifties stood talking to a nurse.

'Can I help you?' he asked.

'We're from the police,' said Fitzjohn, holding up his warrant card and introducing himself and Betts. 'We're here to inquire about a woman by the name of Constance Parsons whom, we understand, was admitted this evening.'

'Ah, yes. I'm Dr Williamson, her attending physician, Chief Inspector. I'm afraid, at this stage, there's little I can tell you. She hasn't regained consciousness after suffering blunt force trauma to the right side of her skull. She's in a comatose state, I'm afraid. We're doing everything we can for her but to be honest, it doesn't look hopeful, I'm afraid.'

'I see,' replied Fitzjohn as Constance Parsons' effervescent and cheerful nature, when they had met, came to mind. 'We'll come back in the morning, doctor. Hopefully, you'll have some positive news for us.'

As the doctor returned to the desk and resumed his conversation with the nurse, Fitzjohn looked at his watch. 'We can't do anything more tonight, Betts. Let's call it a day and continue on in the morning.'

'I have my examination first thing in the morning, sir,' said Betts as they re-entered the elevator. 'For placement on the promotion list.'

'Ah, right. So you do. Thanks for reminding me.'

'I thought it might be a good opportunity for Smithers to step in for a day,' Betts continued. 'He's nothing but keen.'

'That's what we need,' said Fitzjohn although his thoughts went to Grieg and his conversation with Peta Ashby concerning Smithers. Was Smithers genuinely keen or was this the opportunity he and Grieg had been waiting for? 'At least he'll have the opportunity he wants because I plan to interview the theatre's security guard in the morning as well as attending a search of Dolores Madden's home.'

'Will you also be speaking to Madelaine Wells?' asked Betts as they walked out of the hospital into the darkness.

'No. You and I will do that together, after your examination.'

CHAPTER 14

fter a restless night of concern for Constance Parsons' welfare, Fitzjohn rose early and while his sister Meg slept, he crept downstairs anxious to take advantage of the stillness he found the pre-dawn offered. He hesitated as he emerged from the house into the early morning light and took in the air, made fresh from the rain during the night. As he stepped off the porch to make his way down the garden path, he glanced over the hedge into Rhonda Butler's garden, curious to see the half-built greenhouse and whether she had heeded his advice concerning the cannabis seedlings. With her garden still in shadow, however, it would have to wait until after he had tended his orchids.

The hinges on his glass door of the greenhouse creaked as it swung open emitting a rush of warm, humid air coupled with a strong earthy smell. Closing the door behind him, he switched on the light and gave an involuntary sigh as the shadowy interior was transformed into a sea of colour. His thoughts, however, would not still as he tended each plant. His concern was for Constance Parsons, thrust by circumstance into the murky world of crime and now fighting for her life. Would she survive?

This thought, tinged by guilt, stayed with him until his attention was taken by the sun glinting through the trees, its warmth radiating onto the glass roof and promising a fine day. With this in mind, he opened the air vents and, satisfied that all was well, emerged into the fresh air and started back through the garden to the house. As he made his way, he glanced again over the hedge only to find Rhonda's sister, Adele Carter, peering at him with a wide smile. Wearing a garish flowing gown and with her wavy greyish hair swept up and tied with a bright red scarf, his thoughts went back to the dire consequences of the last time she had visited her sister.

'Mr Fitzjohn. How are you?' she yelled out. 'You remember me, don't you?'

'I do indeed, Ms Carter.'

'Now, now, remember what I told you the last time I was here. My friends call me Blossom and so must you. Still looking after those orchids, I see,' she added, her gaze going to the greenhouse. 'I seem to remember you promised to show them to me. Before events more or less took over, that is,' she added with a chuckle.

Fitzjohn cringed not only at the mention of taking Blossom on a tour of his greenhouse but the "event" as she put it. A fire that had all but destroyed Rhonda's home, started, he suspected, by Blossom falling asleep while smoking a cigarette. Or so it had been thought at the time. Fitzjohn, however, remained in doubt as to the cigarette's specific content, convinced that Blossom preferred cannabis. Which brings the question as to what she thinks of Rhonda's choice of plants, he said to himself. Surely she must be aware it's marijuana.

Deciding to ignore mention of a tour, Fitzjohn said, 'Here on holiday are you?' as he looked past Blossom to the garden bed in question.'

'Yes, just for a few days,' replied Blossom, following Fitzjohn's gaze before moving to block his view.

'In that case, perhaps I can enlist your help in a matter concerning your sister,' he said.

'And what would that be?'

'It concerns the marijuana she's cultivating in that garden bed.'

'Marijuana?' Blossom swung around. 'And I thought you knew all about gardening. You're mistaken, Mr Fitzjohn. They're seedlings for her nephew's school project. Flowers of some description.'

'It's true there are a few geranium seedlings planted,' replied Fitzjohn, 'but if you look a little closer, I believe you'll see there are marijuana seedlings dispersed amongst them. No doubt waiting to be transferred to that new greenhouse once it's finished.'

'That can't be right. Rhonda's too strait-laced to grow pot,' said Blossom with a snicker.

'Other than the geraniums, I'm sure she has no idea what she's growing, Ms Carter, but I have it on good authority that the said seedlings are definitely marijuana. Furthermore, I've had one of my officers consult the headmaster at her nephew's school and there isn't a horticultural school project. Your sister's nephew is using her and in a dangerous way because, as you're no doubt aware, there is a hefty penalty, perhaps jail time, for growing an illicit drug, not to mention being complicit in its ongoing sale.'

'But Rhonda's an upstanding, honest citizen,' replied Blossom.

'Even so, the law will apply, so please try to convince her to get rid of the plants immediately. Otherwise, the drug squad will more than likely be her next visitors and you may find yourself charged with being an accessory.'

'You're not serious,' said Blossom, a horrified look on her face.

'I've never been more serious in my life.' As he spoke, Fitzjohn heard the side gate open and turned to see Constable Smithers, his expressionless pale grey eyes and insipid countenance providing no hint of his belligerent temperament beneath.

∾

'Ah, good morning, Smithers,' said Fitzjohn as a sense of vigilance took hold. 'I understand we're working together today but you're far earlier than I expected. If you wait in the car, I'll be with you shortly.'

'Very well, sir,' replied Smithers, his attention moving to Blossom. As their eyes met, she put her cigarette to her lips and inhaled, releasing several rings of smoke before she turned and disappeared into the house. 'I didn't wish to interrupt but is there trouble with your neighbour, sir?'

'Merely a domestic matter, Smithers. Nothing to worry yourself about,' replied Fitzjohn as he looked into Smithers' smarmy face.

∾

Reluctantly facing a day with Smithers, Fitzjohn left his

cottage and made his way to the waiting car. 'I assume DS Betts has brought you up to speed concerning the murder of Dolores Madden and the attack on Constance Parsons at the Adelphi Theatre last night,' he said, sliding into the passenger seat.

'He has, sir.'

'Good. So you're aware that DS Betts and I were in attendance at the theatre at the time the security guard, Gordon Bennett, prepared to secure the building in readiness for its demolition.'

'Yes, sir. Is that where we're headed now? To the theatre.'

'No,' replied Fitzjohn. 'There's nothing more we can do there. I want to start the day by speaking to Mr Bennett in the hope he can shed light on how these two women came to be in the building. He lives in Roselle. We'll make our way there now.'

Smithers turned the car onto a narrow, tree-lined street before he pulled over to the curb in front of an old terrace house, its rusting iron lattice work and peeling paint providing a backdrop for the shutter that hung precariously by a single hinge on the edge of the front window.

'Mr Bennett doesn't appear to be particularly house proud,' said Smithers as he ran a critical eye over the building and sniffed his disapproval as they approached the front door.

Fitzjohn did not respond. Instead, he moved ahead of Smithers and knocked on the door. It opened almost immediately to reveal Gordon Bennett in bare feet and dressed in a pair of black track pants and an undershirt. He stared at the two officers and removed the cigarette that hung from his lower lip.

'Good morning, Mr Bennett,' said Fitzjohn amicably. 'As you may remember, we last met at the Adelphi Theatre late yesterday afternoon. My sergeant and I left as you closed the building in readiness for the demolition team's arrival today.'

'Of course I remember,' replied Bennett with a degree of scepticism. 'Why, is there a problem?'

'Yes, I'm afraid there is. May we come in?'

Bennett did not reply but moved back from the doorway and the two officers stepped inside. 'Come through,' he said, leading the way into a small living room, its bare wooden floor boards and sparse furnishings lending an uncomfortable feel. Bennett turned off the television and gestured to the sofa before stubbing out his cigarette into an ashtray already overflowing with butts. 'So, what is the problem?' he asked as he sat down in the only available chair.

Ignoring Bennett's question, Fitzjohn asked, 'When we met prior to the theatre's closure, you mentioned that I wasn't the only last-minute visitor you'd had that day and that Simon Roach had also called in.'

'That's right, he did. He said he wanted to take photographs of the auditorium.'

'Did you see him leave, Mr Bennett?'

'No. Does it matter?'

'Yes, it does because I'm trying to find out who might have been in the theatre after it was finally locked up. Did you, by any chance, go back inside after Sergeant Betts and I left?' Bennett did not respond. 'Well?' asked Fitzjohn.

'Yes,' said Bennett at last with a degree of hesitation. 'I went back to get my jacket.'

'I see. And you left the stage door unlocked while you went to retrieve it?'

'Of course. I only planned to be there for a minute or two.'

'And was that the case?' Bennett shifted in his chair. 'How long were you inside, Mr Bennett?' asked Fitzjohn again, his gaze on Bennett intense. 'Mr Bennett, as you know, I'm the investigating officer into the death of Howard Greenwood. I am now also the investigating officer into another homicide that occurred at the theatre last night.'

'*Another?*'

'Yes. Dolores Madden's body was found late last night along with another woman who is clinging to life in the hospital.'

'But…'

'Did you know Dolores Madden was still in the building? Is that why you returned?'

'No. I didn't know she was still there when I locked up, I swear. I found out when I went back in to get my jacket. I heard a noise and went to investigate. I found her in the costume department. I told her I was closing up and she'd have to leave but she begged me to let her stay for a while. In the end, I gave in and let her have a key and asked her to promise to lock the door when she left. I swear she was alive when I left her.' His face was pale, and he ran his hand through his thinning hair. 'Look if this gets out, I'll lose my job with the security company.'

'I think that's the least of your problems right now,' muttered Smithers under his breath.

Ignoring Smithers' snide remark, Fitzjohn asked, 'How long were you in the costume department with Dolores, Mr Bennett?'

'Ten minutes or so. I think she wanted someone to talk to because she was upset about the theatre's closure.' Bennett looked Fitzjohn in the eye. 'I didn't kill her, Chief Inspector. You've got to believe me.' His hand shaking, Bennett grabbed a cigarette from the pack on the small table next to his chair and put it between his lips, trying to steady his hands as he lit up.

'If I were Bennett, I wouldn't be worrying about my job, I'd be more concerned with being charged with murder,' said Smithers as the two officers emerged from the house.

'But you're not Mr Bennett, Smithers, and whatever your thoughts are on the matter, it's less than professional to voice them while conducting an interview,' replied Fitzjohn as they reached the car.

'Well it seems to me that either Bennett or Roach killed Dolores Madden,' replied Smithers, disregarding Fitzjohn's comment.

'You're forgetting means, motive and opportunity,' said Fitzjohn. 'Bennett had the opportunity, but we would have to connect the murder weapon to him, not to mention his motive for the killing. And as far as Roach is concerned, we're yet to determine whether he was still in the building. It all takes time, Smithers. You can't hurry these things. After all, you might incriminate the wrong person.' Doubting that anything he said would penetrate the apparent superior nature of Smithers' disposition, and considering his presumed alliance with Grieg, Fitzjohn fell silent, disinclined to discuss the case further.

'Are we going to speak to Simon Roach now?' asked Smithers as he merged the car into the traffic.

'No. I want to look in on the search that Senior Constable Williams is conducting on Dolores Madden's apartment.'

The two officers arrived at Dolores' apartment building a short time later. In stark contrast to the previous premises they had attended, Dolores' abode was contained in a relatively small and neat complex which had been enhanced by a leafy garden. On entering the building, Fitzjohn, followed by Smithers, climbed the stairs to the landing above to find her apartment door open.

He stepped into the living room amid the team of police officers conducting the search and, despite its small space, it became obvious that the costume director had held dear her years in the theatre. With a host of posters depicting past plays performed at the Adelphi displayed on the rose-coloured wall to the right, the vision of memorabilia continued on the opposite wall with a collage of photographs taken throughout its history. Leaning forward over the sofa, its surface a mass of brightly coloured cushions, he studied each snapshot of past and more recent performers, along with others vital to each production. As he did, he looked for a likeness of the victim, Howard Greenwood. Not surprisingly, he thought, Dolores chose not to display a photograph of the man who had, on so many occasions, threatened to have her dismissed. As this thought crossed his mind, he found Smithers at his side.

'How anyone could live in the midst of this clutter is

beyond me,' he said, running his critical eye around the room. 'I'm a minimalist myself.'

'We each have our own preferences when it comes to décor,' said Fitzjohn, 'and besides, we're not here to pass comment or to judge Ms Madden's living arrangements, we're here merely in our capacity as police officers to conduct our investigation and I suggest you do just that.' As Smithers flounced off towards the kitchen, Fitzjohn made his way to the apartment's master bedroom where he found Senior Constable Williams.

'Have you found anything at all that could be relevant to the case, Williams?' he asked.

'Not yet, sir.'

'Very well, carry on,' replied Fitzjohn as he turned to take in the room. Again, its décor inspired a certain warmth with its colourful cushions, a bright blue shawl resting on the bed while multihued scarves were hung on hooks and laid across an armchair in the corner. The open closet door revealed an array of vibrant coloured gowns while shoes were neatly stored on the closet floor. Even the glass in the window that overlooked the street below had not escaped Dolores's embellishment with stars of various dimensions stuck to the glass. No doubt clothes and their accessories were an important part of Dolores Madden's existence, he thought, as he noticed a number of leather handbags all but filling a large basket against the far wall. Fitzjohn bent to examine them until he heard Williams call out.

'It looks like we have something here, sir, hidden underneath the bed.'

As Williams spoke, one of the officers in the room pulled a briefcase out, the lid falling back to expose rows of bank notes held tightly together with rubber bands.

Reluctant to discuss what had been unearthed in Dolores Madden's apartment, or the possible implications it might have on the case, Fitzjohn steered the conversation to what Smithers' hopes and aspirations were concerning his career in the police force. Given the opportunity to talk about himself, Smithers responded with enthusiasm until he turned the car into the parking area at the rear of the station.

'Thank you, Smithers,' said Fitzjohn. 'I hope today has given you an inkling into what you can expect if you decide to embark on a career as a detective. I'll let you know if I need anything further from you.'

'I thought I'd do a background check on Gordon Bennett, sir.'

'Thank you but I need to consult DS Betts on the matter first. He's due back shortly so if we decide to go ahead, you'll be advised.' Fitzjohn gave a quick smile and continued on into the station, a feeling of relief that he had at least satisfied the man's request to play a part in the investigation. Now that had been accomplished, he need not have anything more to do with him. Opening his office door, he entered and switched on the light. At the same time, Betts appeared behind him in the doorway.

'Ah, how did the examination go?' asked Fitzjohn as he shrugged out of his suit coat and settled himself into his chair.

'I think it went well, sir. Now I just have to wait to hear whether or not I'm found eligible for placement on the promotion list.'

'You meet all the criteria, so I'm confident you don't have anything to worry about,' replied Fitzjohn. 'What's this?' he continued as Betts placed a folder on his desk before he sat down.

'It's the background check on Stephanie Mowbray, sir. I've read through it and it's as she said, she and Howard Greenwood met while they were at acting school almost twenty-five years ago. What she didn't mention, however, is that at the time they were engaged.'

'Ah, so they were romantically involved. I wonder what happened to alter that.'

'Marsha happened, sir, the victim's now deceased wife. She arrived at the school in the second semester and, not long after her arrival, Howard broke off his engagement to Ms Mowbray.'

'So that might explain the real reason Stephanie Mowbray decided an acting career was not for her. Instead, she pursued dress designing.'

'It could be although it seems that she never lost touch with the victim. In fact, she eventually became his wife's favoured dress designer and friend,' said Betts.

'I wouldn't have thought that would have been easy for her under the circumstances but perhaps with the passage of time she realised their relationship wouldn't have worked. Did she ever marry?'

'No, sir.

'Mmm. Well, with that situation in mind, I think there's good reason she remains a person of interest in Howard Greenwood's murder with her motive being one of jealousy after he slighted her.'

'But surely she wouldn't still hold a grudge after so much time,' said Betts.

'You wouldn't think so but it is possible. People have been

known to hold a grudge for a lifetime and remember, revenge is best served cold.'

'But if that's how she really felt, I don't see how she could hide it from the victim or his wife, sir.'

'She may or may not have been successful at doing that, but it wouldn't matter. As we know, Howard Greenwood thought his wife had been murdered. I believe he would keep anyone he thought could be her killer close by until he was ready to reveal who it was. And as far as Stephanie Mowbray is concerned, the situation would have suited her if she is, in fact, his killer. We also need to speak to her again to find out where she was at the time of Madden's murder.'

'How did everything go with Smithers?' asked Betts. 'I know you weren't keen on working with him.'

'It went okay. We attended the search of Dolores Madden's apartment and he accompanied me when I spoke to the security guard, Gordon Bennett, so I think that satisfied his wish to participate in the investigation. He did suggest he do a background check on Bennett, but I'd sooner not include him in any additional work on the case.' Fitzjohn caught Betts' questioning look but chose not to carry the subject further.

'Was anything found in Madden's apartment that will help our case?' asked Betts.

'As a matter of fact there was. You said Dolores Madden's background check revealed she wasn't flushed with money and yet we found thousands of dollars stashed away in a briefcase under her bed, of all places. No doubt from ill-gotten gains otherwise it would surely be in her bank account.' Fitzjohn's thoughts went back to witnessing Dolores rifling through the dresser in Howard's dressing room and thinking she was pilfering when he noticed her slip something into her pocket. 'The question is, how did she come by the money?' he continued. 'Hopefully the lab will come up with a clue.'

'And as far as Bennett is concerned, I didn't mention it at the time but the reason I was anxious to speak to him is because yesterday, while you were meeting with the headmaster, he happened to mention that Simon Roach had returned to the theatre that afternoon to take photographs of the auditorium. Consequently, since this latest murder I asked him whether he saw Roach leave again. He didn't.' Fitzjohn recounted the remainder of his conversation with Bennett. 'We already know Simon Roach had a strong motive where Howard Greenwood's murder is concerned in being threatened with ruin if he carried on with his lawsuit in relation to the plagiarism of his play. If he knew about Howard's memoir, as I suspect he did, it could have been the catalyst that sent him over the edge, believing Howard might twist the truth and blacken his reputation.'

'In which case, as he was witnessed entering the theatre yesterday afternoon, it lends itself to the possibility that the target was Constance Parsons, and Dolores Madden just happened to be in the wrong place at the wrong time,' said Betts.

'It's possible because if he knew about the writing of the manuscript he might also have known Howard had employed a ghost writer.' Fitzjohn thought for a moment. 'Of course, there's also the possibility that, since the stage door was left unlocked while Bennett was in the building, someone else entered while he was talking to Madden in the costume department. Pure speculation, but that someone could have been there concerning the money found in her apartment. See what else you can find out about Madden's life in general, Betts. Talk to the cast and crew again and those she liaised with about costumes. But for now, let's speak to Simon Roach again.'

It was late in the afternoon when the two officers arrived in Cremorne and parked their car outside Simon Roach's home. Fitzjohn looked out through the passenger window at the century old recently restored house, its decorative lead-light windows and wide corner veranda lending a welcoming old-world charm. The front door opened as they approached through the garden.

'Mr Roach, you no doubt remember we spoke the other day,' said Fitzjohn as Roach stood in the doorway. 'We'd like to have another word if we may.'

'I was just on my way out, but I can spare a few minutes, I guess,' replied Roach, gesturing to the wicker chairs on the wide veranda as he closed and locked the front door. 'I doubt, however, I can tell you anything more about my recollection of the after-show party,' Roach continued as he sat down with a confident air.

'We're not here about that, Mr Roach,' said Fitzjohn. 'We're here regarding your whereabouts late yesterday afternoon.'

'My whereabouts? Can I ask why?'

'Because there have been two more incidents at the Adelphi Theatre in the last twenty-four hours. A homicide and an attack causing grievous bodily harm.'

'You're not serious.' Roach grimaced. 'Do I know these people?'

'Dolores Madden whose body was found along with

another woman by the name of Constance Parsons. She's been hospitalised and not expected to live.'

'I know of Dolores. I think I mentioned to you previously that Howard had a particular dislike for her.'

'And the other woman?' asked Fitzjohn.

'Parsons. The name rings a bell. Ah, yes, I know. Isn't she the writer who was helping Howard with his book?'

'So you knew about that?' said Fitzjohn.

'Yes, but not through Howard. He never mentioned it but it appeared to be common knowledge around the theatre.' Simon paused. 'I still don't know why you're here questioning me.'

'We're here because we're led to believe you entered the Adelphi Theatre at approximately four o'clock yesterday afternoon.' Roach glared at Fitzjohn. 'Is that so?' asked Fitzjohn when Roach did not reply.

'Well, yes. I went there to take photographs of the auditorium. I thought it was an opportunity to get some good shots before the place is pulled down. Look, I hope you don't think I had anything to do with what happened.'

'How long were you there?' asked Fitzjohn, ignoring Roach's comment.

'I don't know - half an hour or so.'

'Was photography your only reason for being there?' Roach swallowed hard. 'Was it?' asked Fitzjohn again.

'Yes, of course it was.'

'Are you sure?' Again, Roach did not reply. 'This is a murder investigation, Mr Roach so it is in your best interest to answer our questions truthfully.'

Roach cleared his throat before he said, 'It's complicated. You wouldn't understand.'

'Well, we'll try if you explain,' replied Fitzjohn. 'Take your time. We're in no hurry.'

Roach hesitated, a look of exasperation across his face. 'All right, if you must know, it was to do with a lawsuit I'm bringing against Howard, although now it'll be against his estate. It's a case of plagiarism. He stole my work and I want recompense.' When no response came from Fitzjohn, Roach said, 'It's true. You can speak to my lawyer if you don't believe me.'

'Even though you've sought legal action, it still doesn't explain your reason for going to the theatre,' said Fitzjohn.

'That's true, I suppose, and I can't really explain why I did other than the fact I tend to be pedantic. I wanted to make sure copies of the play he'd plagiarised hadn't been left lying around in his dressing room.'

'Did you find anything?' asked Fitzjohn.

'No.'

'While you were at the theatre, did you see anyone else other than the security guard?' Roach's eyes darted between the two officers. 'Did you?' Fitzjohn asked again.

'As a matter of fact, I did. Despite what you might think, I did take photographs of the auditorium and that's when I saw her.'

'Who?' asked Fitzjohn, his interest piqued.

'Madelaine Wells. She was sitting in the auditorium when I walked onto the stage. At least I think it was her. It was only for a second, mind. When I looked again, she'd gone.'

'What time would that have been?' asked Fitzjohn.

'It wasn't long after I'd arrived. Just after four, I'd say. Before I went to Howard's dressing room.'

'So, you took photographs of the auditorium and searched the dressing room, after which you left the theatre.'

'That's right.'

'Approximately what time did you leave?' asked Fitzjohn.

'Around four-thirty.'

'Did you speak to the security guard before you left?'

'No, he wasn't around.'

'And where did you go after that?'

'I came straight home.'

'Is there anyone who can confirm what time you arrived here?'

'I doubt it unless one of my neighbours happened to see me. I think I mentioned to you before that I live here alone.'

'What do you think?' asked Betts as the two officers left Simon Roach and returned to their car.

'On the two occasions we've spoken to Mr Roach, he's mentioned seeing Madelaine Wells,' replied Fitzjohn as he slid into the passenger seat. 'The first time in the laneway as he left the theatre after the farewell party and the second, last night when he went into the auditorium to take photographs. Of course, if he is the killer, he could be lying in an effort to steer us in the wrong direction. Either way, we need to speak to Wells to ascertain where she was around four o'clock yesterday.'

'What about his reason for being at the theatre, sir? Do you believe him?'

'Do you?' asked Fitzjohn, turning to his young sergeant.

'No because I don't think his story about looking for something relating to his plagiarised play makes any sense, even if he is pedantic,' replied Betts. 'What would make more sense is if he had told us he was looking for the manuscript for Howard's biography, or papers relating to it. But I guess he wouldn't want to admit to that since it could be construed that he lured Constance Parsons to the theatre.'

'That's right. But for any of that to be useful we need hard evidence,' said Fitzjohn as Betts pulled away from the curb. 'Have Roach's phone records checked to see if he telephoned the bookshop. Also, have a check done on all incoming calls the bookshop landline has received in the last week.' Fitzjohn fell silent for a moment as his thoughts returned to Constance Parsons. 'When we get back to the station, I'll contact the hospital to find out whether there's been any change in Ms Parsons' condition but first, let's pay Stephanie Mowbray another call. Since we know she had a strong motive to kill Greenwood, I'd like to know where she was at the time of Dolores Madden's death.'

Fitzjohn and Betts arrived at The Strand Arcade and made their way up the tiled staircase to the balcony that encircled the upper level. The bell on the shop door tinkled when they entered the quiet space to find a young sales woman behind the counter.

'Hello, can I help you?' she asked.

'We're from the police, miss,' said Fitzjohn, presenting his warrant card. 'We'd like to speak to Stephanie Mowbray, if we may. Is she in?'

'No, she isn't, I'm afraid.'

'Do you know when she'll be back?' asked Fitzjohn.

'I have no idea, Chief Inspector. I haven't seen her since I arrived for work yesterday afternoon at two o'clock. She left soon after and hasn't been back since.'

'I see. Do you have a mobile number we can reach her on?'

'I do.' The young woman took a business card from a small pile on the counter and handed it to Fitzjohn. 'Her mobile number is at the bottom, but I think you'll find she has it turned off. I've been trying to contact her, with no success, since last evening because I have a problem with one of our suppliers.'

'How late were you open for business last night?' asked Fitzjohn.

'I closed the shop at six, but I was here arranging stock until ten o'clock. I thought Stephanie might return, but she didn't. When she does call in, I'll let her know you want to speak to her.'

'Well, we've learnt one thing,' said Fitzjohn as the two men retraced their steps and returned to their car. 'Stephanie Mowbray wasn't at her place of business when Dolores Madden was murdered, and an attempt made on Constance Parsons' life. See what you can do to locate her, Betts, and have her brought in for questioning.'

'Yes, sir.'

CHAPTER 15

*A*s his taxi wended its way into the city the following morning, Fitzjohn's thoughts went to Rhonda Butler. With the situation relating to her gardening pursuit remaining unresolved, his concern had intensified as its implications resonated in his mind's eye. At the same time, his thoughts were also occupied by his investigations into the Greenwood and Madden murders as well as Stephanie Mowbray's sudden disappearance. Reminding himself of the roses she had mysteriously received, he wondered if she had fallen victim to the killer or was she the killer? Either way, with the predator still at large and Constance Parsons' condition unchanged, how could he ensure her continued safety? This thought persisted to nag at the fringes of his mind as he emerged from the car to feel the brunt of the wind that whipped at his overcoat, his vision marred by his rain splattered glasses. Waving to the distorted image of the constable on duty behind the desk, he hastily released the security door and went straight to his office. Removing his damp overcoat, he sat down heavily into his chair, removed his glasses and gave an exasperated sigh before wiping off the rain drops. At that moment, Betts walked into the room.

'Ah, good morning, Betts. Any news?'

'Yes, sir, the results are back from the lab on the plastic wrapped newspaper. The analysis on the plastic from the victim's skin matches that wrapped around the newspaper and has been confirmed as the murder weapon.'

'What about fingerprints?' asked Fitzjohn.

'They're there, sir, but smudged.'

Fitzjohn sat back in his chair. 'That's a shame but I guess it would've made things too easy, wouldn't it? Any luck on Stephanie Mowbray's whereabouts?'

'Not yet, sir, but hopefully it's just a matter of time. I have Williams and Carruthers working on it. On the positive side, however, I've done a little more digging and found that she has been withdrawing fairly large amounts of money from her bank account on a regular basis for about a year. It made me think of the money you found in Dolores Madden's apartment.'

'In what way?' asked Fitzjohn.

'Well, supposing Dolores was blackmailing Mowbray.'

'Why would she do that?' asked Fitzjohn as he took the papers from his briefcase and set them out in neat piles across his desk.

'Because, if we take into account Marsha Greenwood's death, which her husband believed to be murder, and we assume that Dolores witnessed Stephanie push Marsha down those stairs, it could add up to blackmail.'

'That would explain the money Dolores had stashed and the motive for her murder plus the withdrawals from Mowbray's bank account,' said Fitzjohn. 'But what about the attack on Constance Parsons?'

'If Mowbray knew about the manuscript, and that Constance Parsons was Howard Greenwood's ghost writer, just that fact would mean she's a threat,' replied Betts.

'Mmm. Well it all fits together and, come to think of it, I happened to notice a few items during my search of Madden's home that puzzled me. Amongst them a number of scarves and a shawl with designs along the same lines as those I remember seeing in Mowbray's shop window. If you're right and she was blackmailing Stephanie Mowbray she might have been making the most of her power over Mowbray. It's a scenario we can't ignore but at the same time, we can't overlook our other persons of interest. The victim's brother, Leo Greenwood, for instance. He had a strong motive to kill his brother.'

'He did, sir, but I can't see what motive he'd have concerning Madden's death, so I did some further checking and he was at his restaurant, The Salty Oyster, from three o'clock that afternoon until midnight on the day she died. A number of his staff have attested to that fact.'

'On the other hand, Simon Roach has admitted being at the Adelphi Theatre that afternoon at around four o'clock,' continued Betts. 'It's possible he didn't leave twenty minutes later as he claims.'

'True. And it does fall in line with what Gordon Bennett, the security guard told me. He admitted he didn't see Roach leave the building.' Fitzjohn thought for a moment. 'So what you're saying is Roach could have planned to kill Constance Parsons because of her knowledge of the memoir and Dolores Madden got in the way.'

'Yes, sir.'

'It's possible but then again, Roach might be telling the truth and he did leave. It might also be true that he saw

Madelaine Wells in the auditorium in which case she could be our killer.'

We still need to find out her movements that evening. Why don't you do that while I call into the hospital to check on Constance Parsons again. Hopefully there'll be a positive change that might help us.'

~

As Fitzjohn made his way up to the intensive care unit of the hospital, a rush of memories surfaced in his mind as he emerged from the elevator, memories of his late wife, Edith, and her last days in this very place.

'Can I help you?'

Jolted from his thoughts, Fitzjohn approached the nurses' station and introduced himself. 'I'm here to inquire about the condition of a patient by the name of Constance Parsons. She was admitted two days ago.'

'She's no longer with us, Chief Inspector.' Fitzjohn took a sudden intake of breath. 'She's been moved upstairs to a private room. Level six.'

'Oh. So, her condition has improved?'

'Yes,' replied the nurse with a smile. 'She regained consciousness in the early hours of this morning and I'm told she's resting comfortably.'

'That's good to hear,' said Fitzjohn with a sense of relief. 'Thank you, nurse.'

After making his way to level six, Fitzjohn was escorted by the nurse on duty to a room at the end of the hallway where a constable sat outside the door.

'The patient appears to be awake, Chief Inspector,' said the nurse after peaking into the room, 'but please don't stay too long. Rest is what Ms Parsons needs at this time.' With a quick smile the nurse left.

After tapping on the door, he walked into the dimly lit room where Constance lay propped up in bed.

'Ms Parsons, I hope you don't mind the intrusion, but I came to see how you are.'

'Not at all, Chief Inspector, I'm glad you're here. I've been so worried.' As Fitzjohn neared the bed his gaze fell upon a vase full of long-stemmed red roses. 'They were here when I woke up,' she said with an unfamiliar edge to her voice. 'First the scent of roses in the bookshop and now roses just like the ones I saw thrown over Dolores's body.'

'I'll have you moved to another part of the hospital, Ms Parsons.'

'I doubt it would make much difference, do you? I believe whoever this person is will find me wherever I go.'

'Not necessarily but I won't hide the fact that the situation is serious so we have to take every precaution we can,' said Fitzjohn as he sat down at the bedside. 'I'll make sure your whereabouts are not recorded on the hospital's database and I'll double the guard on your door.'

'That's good of you,' replied Constance. 'I know you're trying to help and I do appreciate it. This whole thing is my fault, of course. I should never have gone to the theatre in the first place. It was stupid of me.'

'Why did you go?' asked Fitzjohn.

'I went because I got a telephone call from your sergeant saying you wanted me to meet you there. At least I thought it was him at the time. Oh, I feel such a fool to have been so gullible. I should have known you wouldn't request such a thing. But then, I suppose if I hadn't gone, poor Dolores might not have been found for days, or worse, until the building came down.'

'So, it was a man who telephoned you?' asked Fitzjohn.

'Well, that's debatable although it did sound like a man's voice, but muffled.' Constance recounted what had happened when she entered the theatre. 'I don't think I've ever been so frightened in all my life and when I found Dolores like that… I think her image will stay with me forever. I can't say I knew her well. We'd only ever passed the time of day when I went to the theatre to meet Howard about the manuscript but nevertheless… It became clear to me early on that Howard didn't like her. Perhaps she was the one he planned to expose as his wife's killer.'

'Can you remember what time you arrived at the theatre?' asked Fitzjohn.

'Well, let's see. The telephone rang as I was just about to leave the bookshop which was 5:30. The theatre's twenty minutes away so, with the traffic at that time of day, I would have arrived at about six o'clock.'

'Are you able to describe the person who attacked you?' asked Fitzjohn.

'No. There wasn't enough light. All I saw was a shadow before I turned and ran. Much good it did me because I got lost in all those passageways. The only thing I remember is being pushed from behind. I can't think how I came to be here and more to the point, alive.'

'You were found by the foreman of the demolition team. We believe he must have disturbed whoever attacked you.'

After seeing to the change in Constance's location within the hospital and securing further protection for her, Fitzjohn reluctantly returned to the station with a sense of unease. Clearly, the killer knew her whereabouts and would strike again. With this in mind, he put a succession of inquiries into motion concerning the source by which the long-stemmed red roses had been delivered to her hospital room. While he waited for news, he entered the deserted incident room and contemplated the images displayed on the whiteboard and considered the adjustments the investigative record of inquiries needed. His thoughts, however, were interrupted as the door at the back of the room opened and Betts walked in.

'Ah, well timed, Betts. How did you get on with the Wells woman? Does she have an alibi for the night Dolores Madden was murdered?'

'She does, sir,' replied Betts as he joined Fitzjohn at the front of the room. 'At the time, she said she was on her way to an audition at the State Theatre. There is a record of her attendance, although it doesn't stipulate the exact time she arrived or left. There were fifty-three hopefuls so Madelaine was just a face in a large crowd.'

'Did she offer the name of anyone who can verify the time she spent at that theatre? Other actors she knows who were also auditioning, perhaps.'

'She did, and I spoke to a young man who said he remembered speaking to her, apparently, just after his audition was finished and as he was leaving the theatre. That was around seven p.m.'

'Was she leaving at that time too?' asked Fitzjohn.

'No, sir.'

'Which means she has no alibi for the time of Dolores Maddens death. According to Charles, it occurred between eight and ten p.m.'

'That's right, and the reason why I decided to make further inquiries about her relationships amongst the cast and crew at the Adelphi Theatre. It wasn't without trouble as far as Dolores Maddens was concerned. Apparently, they didn't get on well. In fact, they had an altercation over a costume the night Howard Greenwood died. One of many, apparently. Evidently, Wells is a bit of a prima donna and was generally not liked, not since she took on the leading female role, that is.'

'So, her animosity towards Dolores is a known fact, but what reason would she have to lure Constance Parsons to the theatre that night?' questioned Fitzjohn.

'The only reason I can think of is that Ms Parsons would be seen as having knowledge of who killed Marsha, if Howard did, in fact, write about it in his memoir. And we know that Madelaine Wells coveted Marsha's role in the play, so she did have a motive to push her down that flight of stairs,' said Betts.

'Unless, of course, Howard Greenwood's assumption is wrong and the coroner's finding is correct. Nevertheless, my instincts tell me that Howard and Dolores Madden's murders are connected. In any event, I think we can eliminate Leo Greenwood from our list of persons of interest since he has a solid alibi for the time of Dolores Madden's death and the attempted murder of Constance Parsons.'

'Which mean we're left with Mowbray, Roach and Wells, sir. Who do you think had the strongest motive in both homicides?'

'Mowbray,' replied Fitzjohn. 'She had been engaged to Howard Greenway before he married Marsha. If she did indeed push Marsha down the stairs and she thought Howard intended to expose that fact, she would also want to silence Constance Parsons since she was the ghost writer of the memoir. And there's also a possibility she was being blackmailed by Dolores who attended the Christmas party.'

'So what you're saying is that Mowbray arranged for Constance Parsons to call in at the theatre in the belief she would be meeting you and Dolores was there by chance,' said Betts.

'It's a possibility if we assume that when she found Dolores in the building, she decided to get rid of that threat as well.' Fitzjohn thought for a moment. 'The only problem with that theory is that Constance Parsons thought the person who lured her to the theatre was a male. She did, however, say that she wouldn't rule out that it was a female.'

'So, Ms Parsons has regained consciousness,' said Betts.

'Yes, and against all odds it seems, but not without a further problem, I'm afraid.' Fitzjohn recounted his conversation with Constance. 'The roses at her bedside when she awoke are particularly disturbing and shows that whoever we're dealing with is not only a killer but cruel.'

'Do you think it could be Roach?' asked Betts.

'That's debatable. We know he had motive concerning the plagiarism of his play but I can't see that it would have driven him to murder,' said Fitzjohn. 'Wells, on the other hand, was sighted in the auditorium, she also has no alibi and by all accounts, she and Dolores didn't get on. Even so, I need to think on it. Any news, as yet, on Stephanie Mowbray's whereabouts?'

'No, sir.'

CHAPTER 16

*I*n the days that followed, Fitzjohn's frustration grew. Not only did Mowbray's whereabouts remain a mystery but inquiries into the roses that had been delivered to Constance Parsons' bedside lingered on without resolution. Fitzjohn threw his pen down on the desk and sat back in his chair before lifting his gaze to see Betts walk into the room.

'I've got news that might brighten your day,' he said.

'And what makes you think my day isn't bright?' asked Fitzjohn, shifting in his chair before shuffling the papers on his desk. 'What news?' he added after a moment's hesitation.

'I took a punt and paid another call to Stephanie Mowbray's shop in the Strand Arcade and she happened to be leaving when I arrived,' said Betts. 'I've had her brought in for questioning. She's in Interview Room 2.'

'So, she didn't fall prey to the killer as I was beginning to think.'

'There was no possibility of that if she turns out to be the killer,' replied Betts.

Fitzjohn and Betts entered the interview room to find Stephanie Mowbray sitting at the table looking down at her iPhone. When the two officers walked in, she slipped the phone back into her handbag.

'Thank you for coming in to talk to us, Ms Mowbray,' said Fitzjohn as he took his seat.

'I didn't have much choice,' replied Mowbray, giving Betts a disparaging glare. Ignoring this, Betts turned on the recording device and sat back in his chair. 'I hope you both realise what an inconvenience you've caused me,' she continued. 'I was on my way to an appointment. Why have I been brought here anyway? I've told you everything I know about Howard's death.'

'That may be the case, Ms Mowbray, however, it's not the reason you've been brought in. This is concerning another matter,' said Fitzjohn. 'We'd like to know where you were on Wednesday, July 11, between the hours of four in the afternoon and midnight.'

'Why?'

'Because at some point during that time period there was a further murder committed at the Adelphi Theatre. I assume you have heard the news.'

'I'm a busy person, Chief Inspector. I rarely get the chance to listen to the news so no, apart from Howard Greenwood's death, I haven't heard about further evils being carried out at the theatre so I can't help you.'

'Nevertheless, it is in your best interest to cooperate and tell us where you were,' said Fitzjohn.

'Not that it's any of your business but if you must know, I was at the Seaview Nursing Home visiting my mother. She has dementia. She's been at the home for the past year. I visit her several times a week, but this week a little more often because she had a turn for the worse. On the day in question, I was there for most of the day and evening. Can I go now?'

'I just have one more question in regard to your bank account,' said Fitzjohn. 'It's been discovered that large sums of money have been withdrawn, in cash, on a regular basis over the past year. Can you explain why?'

'*I don't believe this*,' barked Mowbray, flouncing back in her chair. 'What gives you the right to look into my private affairs?'

'The fact that we're conducting investigations into two murders and one attempted murder, Ms Mowbray,' replied Fitzjohn. 'So, are you going to answer the question?'

'If you must know, the money went to pay for keeping my mother in the nursing home. It doesn't come cheap. Not that you would know anything about that. Now, if you don't mind I've got a business to run.'

'What do you think, sir,' asked Betts as the two officers watched Stephanie Mowbray leave the station. 'She didn't seem too phased at the news of another murder.'

'If she's telling the truth, I regret what we've put her through. But I doubt she is because I'm sure payment would be made electronically through the banks. Check it out, Betts and find out whether she was at the nursing home on Wednesday as she claims.' As Fitzjohn spoke, the duty officer appeared at Fitzjohn's side.

'The chief superintendent wants to see you, sir.'

'Thank you, sergeant.' Fitzjohn turned back to Betts. 'No

doubt she's anxious to hear what progress we've made and, at this point, I'm not sure what I can tell her. Has there been any word on tracing where the roses come from?'

'Not yet, sir. All florists in the metropolitan area have been contacted without success. We're now trying growers, but it's time consuming.'

'And there's always the possibility they're being supplied innocently by a gardening enthusiast who might be an acquaintance of the killer,' said Fitzjohn. 'If that's the case it'll be almost impossible to track down.'

'I'll see what I can find out about individuals who associate with those we suspect, starting with Stephanie Mowbray, sir.'

~

As Betts left for the nursing home, Fitzjohn made his way to Peta Ashby's office where he found her pacing the floor. She stopped when he appeared in the doorway.

'You wanted to see me, ma'am.'

'Yes, Fitzjohn, I do. Come in.' Unsmiling, Peta gestured to a chair and closed the door behind him.

'I apologise for not speaking to you sooner in regard to the more recent homicide and the attack on Constance Parsons at the theatre, but events seemed to have taken over,' said Fitzjohn, sensing Peta's disquiet as he settled himself into the chair.

'Your case isn't what I want to talk to you about,' she replied, sitting down at her desk and clasping her hands together. 'It's...' Peta sighed. 'This is difficult but I'm sure you'll be able to provide me with an explanation.'

'Oh? What is it?'

'An allegation has been lodged against you with internal affairs. It's in regard to your mishandling of a case involving the cultivation of marijuana. I'm sure it's a misunderstanding because to my knowledge, you're not involved in any such investigation, are you?'

'Can I ask who made the complaint, ma'am?'

'That's confidential.'

'In that case, can you tell me exactly how I'm meant to have mishandled the situation?'

'That I can tell you.' Peta looked down at the paperwork in front of her. 'It says here that you are complicit with the person or persons in the cultivation of an illegal substance by not making an arrest. Tell me it's a ridiculous assumption, Fitzjohn, because I need you to refute the allegation in a sworn statement,' said Peta, lifting her gaze to meet Fitzjohn's gaping look.

'I can't do that, ma'am.'

'Do you mean you are investigating a case without my knowledge?' asked Peta in disbelief.

'There is no case nor an investigation although there is a person cultivating an illegal substance, albeit seedlings.'

'For heaven's sake,' barked Peta, her voice raising in volume. 'However advanced these plants are in their growth isn't an issue. The fact that it's true is. You'd better explain.'

Over the next several minutes, Fitzjohn told Peta of Rhonda Butler's new gardening practices and the approach he had decided to take to deal with the situation. 'I've known Rhonda Butler for many years, ma'am, and I was convinced from the outset that she is ignorant as to the species of plant her nephew had asked her to grow. I was also immediately doubtful that its cultivation was for his high school horticultural class which has since been proved correct.'

'It doesn't eliminate the fact that you knew a crime had been committed and didn't take measures to make an arrest,' replied Peta in exasperation. 'The drug squad are on their way to see Mrs Butler as we speak.'

'This has been blown out of all proportion, ma'am,' said Fitzjohn, shaking his head. 'As I said, Mrs Butler is an unsuspecting victim of her nephew, a child of sixteen. Our inquiries have found he had lied to his aunt concerning the reason he needed to use her garden but that only came to light a few hours ago. I would have dealt with the matter appropriately given the time.'

'I'm not here to judge you, Fitzjohn. Given the circumstances your means of handling the situation might have been successful if this complaint hadn't been made against you.'

'It was Smithers, wasn't it?' said Fitzjohn.

'As I said, I'm not at liberty to disclose the name of the person who made the accusation,' said Peta, shifting in her chair. 'But it is my unpleasant task to tell you that as of this moment, you're suspended from duty pending the decision of the Internal Affairs Tribunal.'

'But I'm in the middle of two murder investigations and an attempted homicide, ma'am.'

'I'm sorry, Fitzjohn, I really am but I have to abide by the regulations set down for such cases.' Fitzjohn slumped back in his chair and an awkward silence ensued. 'DS Betts will take over.' As their eyes met, he realised her words severed any possibility of ever telling her his true feelings for her. They were colleagues and that is how it would remain.

~

With a heavy heart, Fitzjohn returned to his office, sat at his desk and tried to take in the fact he was now, officially, suspended from duty. Of course, he knew very well that through Smithers, Grieg had once again succeeded in his quest to end his career in the force. Knowing that Smithers was one of Grieg's minions, he should have been more vigilant but who would have expected he would have taken a conversation with a neighbour and blown it out of all proportion? Sitting back, he looked around, his thoughts going over the many years and cases he had mulled over in the room. Good years and bad, but perhaps it was now at an end.

By the time Betts returned to the station some time later and walked in, he had already placed most of his belongings into a cardboard box that now sat on top of his desk along with his briefcase.

'You look like you're planning on going somewhere, sir,' said Betts somewhat perplexed.

'Take a seat. There's something I need to talk to you about,' said Fitzjohn.

With a questioning look, Betts settled himself into a chair. 'What is it, sir?'

'There's been an unforeseeable development which means a change of routine.' Fitzjohn recounted his conversation with the chief superintendent.

'*Suspended?*' said Betts with a look of astonishment. 'Who made these allegations?'

'The chief superintendent wasn't able to tell me but I have a fair idea. I suspect it was Smithers. Ordinarily, I'd keep this thought to myself but in this case, I think you should know. You see, I've always felt Smithers held allegiance to Inspector

Grieg whose fondest wish is to have my career on the force terminated.'

'I've never said anything, but I am aware of that, sir.'

'I thought you might be,' replied Fitzjohn.

'But where does that leave us with our investigations?' asked Betts.

'The chief superintendent has advised that you're to take over.'

Betts sat straight in his chair. 'I appreciate her confidence in me, sir, but...' Betts swallowed hard.

'You'll do just fine,' replied Fitzjohn. 'However, given the situation and the fact that we've worked together over a number of years, I have one word of warning; be mindful of Smithers.'

'I had no idea he was a snitch for Inspector Grieg. That's why you weren't keen for him to be involved in the case. I'm sorry I suggested it, sir.'

'There's nothing to be sorry about, Betts. I went into it with my eyes wide open and felt everything went fine. I believed I'd managed to satisfy his request to gain some experience. What I didn't realise was that he was on a mission. Not for himself but for Grieg.' Fitzjohn paused. 'Anyway, what's done is done. The important thing now is that you carry on.'

'But how did he gain the information to make the allegations, sir?'

'The only thing I can think of is it was when he arrived at my home the other morning as I was speaking to Blossom about the marijuana seedlings. He must have overheard our conversation before I realised he was there. Obviously, he saw it growing and put two and two together.'

'But from what you told me, you gave Rhonda fair

warning and you gave me instructions to look into her nephew's claims about his school project. In fact, other than our earlier discussion about the case, I also came in here to discuss the next step as far as the nephew is concerned.'

'Well, we would have interviewed him immediately and depending on the result, gone from there, but I'm afraid it's now out of our hands. The drug squad have been called in.' Fitzjohn paused. 'I know I'm no longer involved, but how did you get on at the nursing home?'

'I spoke to a couple of the staff who were on duty last Wednesday and both said they remembered Greta Mowbray had a female visitor throughout the afternoon and evening who matched Stephanie Mowbray's description.'

'Well, it isn't a definite confirmation of her alibi but who else but a family member would spend most of the day visiting? And after meeting Ms Mowbray, I doubt whether anything would keep that woman from her business other than someone dear to her heart.'

'I agree,' replied Betts, 'in which case I'll turn my attention to Madelaine Wells.'

'And I'd better be on my way,' said Fitzjohn as he looked around his office. 'I don't want to drag my leaving out any longer than I have to. You know where you can find me if you have any questions, not that I have the slightest doubt about your investigative abilities, mind. It's just that sometimes two heads are better than one.' Fitzjohn gave a quick smile, picked up his briefcase and the cardboard box and left the room.

It was late afternoon when Fitzjohn opened the front door

and walked into his Birchgrove cottage. As he did, Meg appeared at the end of the hall.

'Alistair, what on earth are you doing home at this time of day?'

'It's a long story,' replied Fitzjohn, placing his briefcase on the hall table and shrugging out of his overcoat before draping it over the banister. 'I'll tell you over a cup of coffee. On second thought, make that a glass of whiskey.'

'It's a bit early for whiskey,' replied Meg, looking at her watch, 'but I think I'll join you after what I've just seen.'

'Why? What's happened?' asked Fitzjohn as he followed his sister into the kitchen.

'I suppose the proper term is a drug bust,' said Meg as she poured the amber liquid into two glasses. 'Men and women in uniform, others in plain clothes. I've never seen such a hullabaloo. Obviously they expected it to be a large narcotic operation, not just a few seedlings. Anyway, they took the poor woman *away*. I think a knock on her door rather than a raid would have been sufficient, Alistair, even though she wouldn't listen to reason.'

'It wasn't my doing,' replied Fitzjohn, 'but it is part of the reason I'm home early.' Fitzjohn ushered Meg through to the conservatory where they sat down. Taking a sip of his whiskey, he paused, feeling its warmth in his throat before he said,' I've been suspended from duty.'

'*What*? Meg choked as the whiskey's warmth hit her throat.

'It's a long and complicated story but the gist of it is that I didn't deal with the matter concerning Rhonda Butler appropriately. Consequently, I was reported to internal affairs.'

'That's appalling,' said Meg wide eyed. 'After all your

years of service to the police department to be treated like this. Don't they even give you the opportunity to defend your actions?' she asked.

'Yes. I'll be able to do that when I appear before the inquiry.' Fitzjohn took another sip of his whiskey. 'I wish it hadn't come to this as far as Rhonda is concerned however.'

'What will happen to her?'

'She'll have been taken in for questioning and, no doubt, will be released on bail but even so, it's harsh treatment for her.'

Long after Meg retired for the evening, Fitzjohn remained in the conservatory mulling over the day's events. Did it mean the end of his career? If so, what did the future hold? But while a myriad of thoughts ran through his mind, one fact remained steadfast. It went against his grain to walk away from an investigation. But his hands were tied. 'Or are they?' he said quietly to himself.

Before dawn the following morning, his decision had been made.

CHAPTER 17

*T*he next morning, dressed in his old gardening clothes, his wire-framed glasses perched on the top of his head, Fitzjohn closed the greenhouse door and made his way along the garden path towards the house, humming a tune as he went. His brief stroll was interrupted, however, when Betts came through the side gate.

'Morning, Betts.'

'Good morning, sir,' Betts replied with a puzzled look.

'I daresay you thought you'd find me in deep despair.'

'Something like that, sir. Aren't you the least bit upset or angry at what's happened?'

'I admit to being angry initially but I gave the whole situation quite a bit of thought overnight and I feel better since I came to a decision. Come inside, I want to know your thoughts because it would involve you.'

Betts followed Fitzjohn into the kitchen where the aroma of brewed coffee filled the air.

'I came to the conclusion that I need to continue with the investigation,' he said as he poured the steaming coffee into two mugs before leading the way into the conservatory. 'And please don't think it's a reflection on your investigative abilities because it isn't. You're more than capable,' he added as they settled themselves into the wicker chairs set in the bay window overlooking the garden. 'It's me. I can't bring myself to walk away from the case.' Fitzjohn took a sip of coffee before he said, 'What I want to ask you is, do you have any objections?'

'No, sir. I'd have been surprised if you hadn't come to this decision.'

'Even though there could be trouble on the horizon if we went ahead? Not for myself because I'm prepared to accept the consequences of my action, but for you, Betts. There's the possibility that you'd be seen as complicit in my activities and it worries me because you have your whole career ahead of you.'

'I know that but at the same time, I don't agree with your suspension, sir, and I daresay I'd do the same if I found myself in your position.'

'Thanks, Betts. I appreciate your support,' replied Fitzjohn.

Betts smiled and lifted his coffee mug in a toast. 'So, we can carry on with our plan to speak to Madelaine Wells. I made a few inquiries and found out she'll be at the State Theatre this morning getting ready for her matinee performance. We can speak to her there rather than have her come into the station.'

'Our first clandestine operation,' said Fitzjohn. 'I never thought I'd have to stoop to such measures.'

Betts peered out of the window into Rhonda's garden. 'On another subject; I heard about Mrs Butler's arrest yesterday.'

'Mmm. I feel responsible,' said Fitzjohn following Betts' gaze. 'It should never have happened. After all, she has no previous convictions other than being a neighbour from hell. Her nephew, of course, is another matter as he organised the cultivation of an illicit drug, albeit with his aunt. Hopefully his age and the fact it is more than likely his first offense will be taken into consideration but nonetheless it's not a good start for a young life. I only hope he's learnt a valuable lesson and straightens out. As far as neighbourly relations go however, I can't see those improving.'

Fitzjohn and Betts arrived at the State Theatre on Market Street in the city and after showing their warrant cards, were escorted backstage to Madelaine's dressing room where the attendant knocked on the door.

'You have visitors, Ms Wells,' he called out.

Moments passed before the door flew open and Madelaine appeared, a fan of long feathers emanating from the headdress she wore, her glittering tight fitting costume revealing every curve. 'What do you want?' she asked, eyeing the two officers from under long false eyelashes.

'We'd like to speak to you again, if we may, Ms Wells,' said Fitzjohn.

'*Now?* That's impossible. I have to go on in a matter of minutes.'

'It won't take long,' said Fitzjohn with a quick smile. He stepped inside as Betts stumbled on the uneven flooring, his eyes agog as they followed Madelaine's retreating figure. 'As I said,' Fitzjohn continued, eyeing Betts, 'we wish to speak to you again but this time it concerns our investigation into the death of Dolores Madden. Her body was found in the costume department of the Adelphi Theatre on Wednesday night.'

'Mmm. I heard about it on the news,' replied Madelaine, sitting down at the dressing table where she began to touch up her makeup. 'The last time I saw her was on closing night. Wait a minute,' she said, spinning around on her chair. 'You aren't thinking I had anything to do with her murder, are you?'

'We're making inquiries into who was at the Adelphi Theatre the day she died, and we have a witness who saw you sitting in the auditorium late in the afternoon. Consequently, we'd like you to explain what you were doing there.'

'The simple answer is, I wasn't there. At that time on that day, I was on my way here for an audition.'

'The Adelphi Theatre is on your way, Ms Wells. Are you sure you didn't call in?' Fitzjohn asked.

'Of course I'm sure.'

'Two minutes, Ms Wells,' came a voice from the hallway.

'Look, I've got to go. I'm due on stage.' Madelaine grabbed a fan of feathers and after a self-admiring pose in the mirror, glided out of the room.

Fitzjohn turned to Betts. 'If you don't close your mouth you're bound to catch a fly,' he said.

'It's hard to believe she'd be capable of murder,' said Betts as the door closed on their way out.

'Don't be deceived by looks and an innocent persona, Betts. She's an actress after all and well-practiced in playing a role. Most people would find the mere fact of being implicated in a murder worrying at the very least, but she doesn't show any sign of concern.'

'It could be she's telling the truth and wasn't at the Adelphi that afternoon,' said Betts.

'And yet Simon Roach is convinced he saw her there,' replied Fitzjohn as the two officers left the theatre and returned to the car.

'But was it her? He could be mistaken.'

'That's true; he could be.' Fitzjohn settled himself into the passenger seat while Betts slid in behind the wheel. 'I think what we need to do before we go any further is consider everything we have concerning both homicides and make a plan for moving forward.'

After arriving at the Charlotte Café, the two officers settled themselves at a table in the far corner and moments later, the waiter arrived with two cups of steaming coffee and a large piece of chocolate cake which he placed in front of Betts. Fitzjohn eyed the cake. 'Is that breakfast?'

'No. I had an egg and bacon roll for breakfast,' replied Betts. 'This is just to get me through till lunch. I'm willing to share, though.'

'That's very kind of you but I don't want to jeopardise my trimmer look,' replied Fitzjohn with a satisfied air. 'It took a lot of sacrifice to get where I am today, not to mention the expense of having all my suits altered down a size. On a more serious note, however, we have a problem if Madelaine Wells is to be believed because it means we no longer have a person of interest in either the Greenwood or Madden homicides, or the attack on Constance Parsons.'

'Well, after some thought, I think Wells did it, sir. She admits she and Howard Greenwood didn't get along and there are those who believe she and Dolores Madden clashed on a regular basis. Plus, it's said she coveted Marsha Greenwood's role in the play before her untimely death.'

'But what threat did Constance Parsons pose?' asked Fitzjohn

'If we assume that Wells did push Marsha Greenwood down those stairs, she would have seen Constance Parsons as privy to whoever Howard Greenwood believed killed her,' replied Betts.

'True enough. Everything does lead to Wells, doesn't it? But there's something not quite right. I feel it in my bones. Perhaps we should speak to Ms Parsons again. You never know, she might have remembered something.'

'Ah, concerning Ms Parsons, sir, I meant to mention that she's being released from the hospital sometime today.'

'Well, that's good news in one sense but it concerns me as far as her safety goes,' replied Fitzjohn. 'See if you can find out whether she'll be returning home or staying with her friend, Harriet Flynn. And I hope it's the latter because with her assailant still on the loose, I don't want her being left alone.'

'I'll see what I can do, sir,' said Betts, getting to his feet.

'What about your cake?' asked Fitzjohn.

'It's tempting but I'd better not. Sophie's been reorganising my diet and chocolate cake isn't on the list. I'll be in touch later today, sir.'

As Betts left, Fitzjohn ordered another cup of coffee and moved to an outside table to enjoy the glimmer of winter sunshine now visible through the clearing sky. As he settled

himself, a myriad of thoughts passed through his mind, not the least of which were the investigations of both homicides as well as the unexpected situation he now found himself in.

'You look miles away, Alistair.' Fitzjohn looked up to see Peta Ashby, 'May I join you?'

'Yes. Please do.' Fitzjohn scrambled to his feet unprepared for the surge of overwhelming feelings for her.

'I'm glad I bumped into you because I've been concerned,' continued Peta as she sat down. 'I know what a distressing situation this must be for you and I want you to know I'm doing everything I can to ensure it doesn't linger on too long. In fact, I believe you'll receive a call in the next day or so because the powers that be want to talk to you.'

'Thanks for letting me know. It's best to be forewarned.' An awkward silence ensued.

'I haven't spoken to DS Betts as yet to find out how he's progressing with the investigations, but I'll do so later today,' said Peta, 'just to see how he's coping and to let him know he has my support.'

'I'm sure he'll appreciate that,' replied Fitzjohn, relieved Peta had not walked in to find he and Betts together because it would have put them both in an awkward position.

'It makes it doubly difficult for you, I imagine,' said Peta. 'With Betts a part of the family, so to speak. Still, I'm sure he'll do the right thing and not discuss the cases with you while things are the way they are.' Fitzjohn did not reply as he wondered if Peta had, in fact, seen Betts leave the café or anticipated there might be collaboration.

Another awkward silence arose before she said, 'There's something else I wanted to speak to you about too, Alistair.'

'Oh?'

'Yes. I realise it's not the right time to bring this up but as

I value your friendship, I feel I must.' Peta bit her lip. 'It's just that for quite some time before these accusations were made against you, we seemed to be getting along so well. It might be my imagination, of course, but the other day, it seemed as though a door closed. Did I say or do something to upset you?'

Fitzjohn shifted in his chair. 'No, you've done nothing,' he replied before his thoughts went back to the speculation amongst those at the station about their relationship. 'At the time, I daresay I was just distracted by the investigations, that's all,' he added, looking down at his empty cup as he fiddled with the teaspoon before he looked up again and met Peta's intense gaze. 'Actually, that's not true. To be honest, I became aware that you and I were a source of rumour and a wager within the station.'

'Concerning what?'

'Our presumed...'

As Fitzjohn spoke, Peta's mobile phone rang. 'I beg your pardon, Alistair, I have to take this. Ashby. Yes, of course. I'm on my way.' Peta hung up and turned back to Fitzjohn. 'I have to go. There's been an incident at the station. I hope we can resume our conversation soon.'

Unsettled by their unexpected encounter and aware he had been on the verge of making his feelings known despite his earlier decision not to, Fitzjohn watched Peta leave the café. Perhaps the interruption was just as well, he thought, since I'm going behind her back and continuing on with my investigations, regardless of my suspension.

Downcast that he had gone behind Peta's back and with a

heavy heart since his feelings for her must remain unsaid, Fitzjohn left the café, making his way home through the leafy suburb as the sun once again disappeared behind a slate grey sky. Inevitably, his thoughts turned to the investigations and the possibility that the murders could remain unsolved and leave Constance Parsons in a perpetual state of peril. This sense of consternation continued for the remainder of the day as he waited to hear from Betts.

'What is wrong with you, Alistair?' asked Meg as she watched him pace the conservatory floor. 'You haven't heard a word I've said, have you?'

Fitzjohn stopped his pacing and turned to face his sister. 'What did you just say, Meg?'

'I said, you haven't heard a word I've been saying,' Meg replied with a degree of exasperation.

'But that's it,' declared Fitzjohn triumphantly. 'It was something she said. I heard it but for some reason, it didn't register until now. Meg, you're marvellous.'

'I'm glad you think so even although I haven't a clue why,' said Meg with a worried look. 'I don't want to upset you, Alistair, but you're not making much sense. It might be a good idea to speak to your doctor. You never know, your suspension could have affected you more than you realise. Perhaps I should ask Martin to phone back later.'

'Is he on the phone?'

'Yes. That's what I came in here to tell you.' Meg handed Fitzjohn his mobile.

'Hello Betts. Were you able to find out what Constance Parsons' plans are when she leaves the hospital?' he asked as his sister left the room.

'Yes, sir. I spoke to Harriet Flynn and she assures me Ms Parsons will be staying with her for her convalescence and until the killer has been apprehended. She's picking her up from the hospital later this afternoon.'

'That's good news, I'm pleased,' said Fitzjohn. 'And what about the roses? Anything yet?'

'So far we've drawn a blank, sir, with no avid gardeners in sight. We'll keep trying. By the way, have you remembered what your bones are trying to tell you?'

'You mean what was causing that feeling in my bones. There is a difference, Betts, and I have, as a matter of fact. It's something Stephanie Mowbray said when we interviewed her at the station. You can verify it by listening to the tape but I'm sure she didn't refer to what happened in the Adelphi Theatre on that Wednesday night in the singular but in the plural, inferring there was more than one incident.'

'Meaning only the killer would know.'

'Exactly.'

'Okay. I'll get onto it, sir, and I'll be in touch.'

CHAPTER 18

Constance emerged from the hospital into the drizzling rain to find Harriet waiting for her beside the car. 'Thank you for coming out on such a miserable day,' she said as she pulled her coat collar up against the wind, her voice still unsteady after her ordeal. 'I do appreciate it as well as your invitation for me to stay with you again.'

'I wouldn't have it any other way,' replied Harriet, opening the car door.

'Be that as it may, I still have my doubts it's a good idea with Howard's killer still on the loose,' replied Constance as she settled herself into the passenger seat. 'I'd never forgive myself if something were to happen to you.'

'Nothing is going to happen to either of us,' replied Harriet in a matter of fact way as she slid into the driver's seat.

'I wish I had your confidence, but I think I lost it when I woke to see those roses at my bedside. It's an indication I'm still a target.'

'I realise how terrifying it must have been for you,

Constance,' said Harriet, pausing before she turned the ignition. 'Let's get you home and into the warmth. I'm sure it'll help you to feel a little better. I laid a fire before I left. There's nothing better than a blazing fire in the hearth on a cold, wet day, is there?'

Little was said as the two women drove through the rain filled streets, Constance lost in her thoughts while Harriet felt concern for her dear friend. She gave a sigh of relief when her old Victorian home came into view, its steep imposing roofline and many gables shadowed by the low-hanging mist giving an air of mystique. Harriet led the way along the garden path to the wide porch and unlocked the front door. Ushering Constance into the living room, she struck a match and lit the fire. Moments later, flames curled and flickered around the logs, adding to the room's ambiance as the flames took hold and sent warmth and light into the room.

'I did plan to offer you a cup of tea as soon as we arrived,' said Harriet as Constance settled herself into an armchair in front of the fire, 'but I've changed my mind. You look like you could do with something a little stronger. A good stiff brandy perhaps?'

'That would be perfect.'

Moments later, Harriet returned carrying two brandy glasses with a good measure of the clear amber fluid in each. Constance sat back and stared into the flames as she took her first sip, feeling the warmth of the liquid in her throat. She flinched at the sudden ring of the doorbell and gave Harriet a fearful look.

'Just drink your brandy and enjoy the fire while I see who that is,' said Harriet, getting to her feet.

'Perhaps we should both go,' replied Constance.

'That won't be necessary. It's more than likely one of my neighbours. After all, killers don't ring doorbells, do they? With that, Harriet disappeared into the front hall and could be heard opening the front door.

'Harriet? Is everything all right?' asked Constance after a long silence followed. When no reply came, she got to her feet and made her way out into the hallway.

'They were lying on the doorstep,' said Harriet, her face drained of colour, her arms holding a spray of long-stemmed red roses.

'The killer knows I'm here,' said Constance.

'I think we should call the chief inspector,' said Harriet, ignoring Constance's remark.

Both Constance and Harriet hovered at the living room window in expectation of the chief inspector's arrival. When a taxi pulled up in front of the house, they both tensed until Fitzjohn's figure could be seen emerging.

'That's odd. I didn't realise the police used the taxi service to make house calls,' said Harriet.

'Neither did I,' replied Constance. 'It must be a sign of the times. Still, it doesn't really matter how he got here, does it? I'm just glad he's finally here. I'll go let him in.'

'Chief Inspector. I can't hide the fact I'm glad you're here,' said Constance as she opened the front door and ushered Fitzjohn inside. As he stepped in, he eyed the spray of roses on the hall table. 'They were left on the doorstep,' she continued. 'By the time Harriet answered the door, whoever left them was gone, I'm afraid. A waste of your time really in the scheme of things.'

'Not in the least, Ms Parson. I'm glad you called to let me know. It's imperative we record every step this predator takes.' The chief inspector paused. 'I know it's disconcerting for you that your whereabouts are known.'

'But not surprising,' replied Constance. 'Whoever it is seems to be able to find me wherever I am.'

'I'll have a word with DS Betts and see what form of protection can be arranged for you both. I'll also ask him to attend so he can view the situation for himself.' The chief inspector hesitated. 'I say that because recent events dictate that I'm no longer involved in the investigations into either the Howard Greenwood or Dolores Madden cases.'

'Oh. I'm sorry to hear that,' replied Constance. 'You have a way of instilling a certain amount of assurance in one that everything will be all right in the end.'

'It still will be, Ms Parsons, because I have every confidence in DS Betts. He's a fine officer. I'll give him a call now and I'll stay with you both until something has been arranged.'

itzjohn sat back in his chair in front of the fire. 'Are you sure you won't have a brandy while you wait for back-up, Chief Inspector?' asked Harriet.

'Really, Harriet, you've been watching far too many crime shows,' said Constance. 'One only needs back-up when one is facing armed criminals of which we're not.'

'That's very kind, Ms Flynn but I think it's best I stick to coffee,' replied Fitzjohn with a smile.

'Of course. Silly of me to suggest it when you're on duty,' said Harriet. Fitzjohn did not reply, choosing not to explain his present state of suspension from the force. 'Oh, I think the troops have arrived,' she continued with a hint of anticipation from her vantage point in front of the bay window. 'A police car and a van with forensic services written on the side.'

'That'll be Sergeant Betts.' Fitzjohn made his way into the hall and opened the front door to find Betts, a young constable and a scene of crime officer.'

'I came as soon as I could, sir,' said Betts, his gaze going to the spray of flowers that rested on the hall table. 'More roses, I see.'

'Yes,' replied Fitzjohn. 'I've explained to the ladies that you're now in charge of the case so you might like to speak to both Ms Parsons and Ms Flynn concerning their delivery.'

'I'll do that, sir.'

'This is Constable Whitelaw,' continue Betts. 'He'll be here on duty throughout the night and will be relieved first thing tomorrow morning.'

Fitzjohn glanced at the constable who hovered nearby. 'Good, because I think the threat is real since Ms Parsons' whereabouts are known.'

'Have you had time to listen to the transcript we recorded while interviewing Stephanie Mowbray?' asked Fitzjohn as the two officers left the house.

'Yes, sir, and you were right. After stating she hasn't heard the news about the homicide on Wednesday, July 11, she clearly states, "I haven't heard about further evils being carried out at the theatre", which suggests she knew there was more than one incident that night.' Betts handed Fitzjohn a copy of the transcript as they settled themselves into the car. 'And as such, I made a few inquiries and I believe we'll find her at her place of business in the Strand Arcade.'

'Good, but before we speak to her again, I'd like a talk with the staff at the nursing home where her mother is living. It might help to give us a bit more background information and, if we're lucky, evidence to go on.'

The two officers arrived at the Seaview Nursing Home to be met by one of the administrative staff. A tall, slender woman in her mid-fifties, her dark brown hair swept into a bun at the nape of her neck, she had intently watched Fitzjohn and Betts through her small office window as they entered the building.

'Good afternoon, gentlemen. I take it you're here to see one of our patients. If you let me have the name, I can point you in the right direction.'

'Thank you, but that's not the case,' replied Fitzjohn as he approached the window. 'I'm DCI Fitzjohn and this is DS Betts. We're conducting investigations into two homicides and...'

'*Homicides!*' interrupted the woman, her attention piqued. 'Heavens above. Surely you don't think any one of our patients could be involved.'

'Not at all, madam, but it will help our investigation if we can speak to whoever has looked after a particular patient over the past year. Her name is Greta Mowbray.'

'Mrs Mowbray? Goodness. Poor woman. She isn't related to one of the victims' is she?'

'No,' replied Fitzjohn.

'The perpetrator then? I can't think which would be worse. How do you think our nursing staff can help you, Chief Inspector?'

'I'm afraid I'm not at liberty to discuss any details with you,' replied Fitzjohn with a growing sense of exasperation.

'No, I suppose not,' replied the woman with a look of disappointment. 'Well, as you seem to be aware, Mrs Mowbray has been with us for the past year so, over that period of time, I'd say most of our nursing staff have looked after her. I'll just go and see who is on duty to speak to you.'

'Perhaps we should have questioned her,' said Betts as the woman bustled off. 'She gives me the impression she's the font of all that goes on in this place.'

'I think you're probably right but for now we'll stick to the nursing staff,' replied Fitzjohn as he walked to the window and took a sweeping look over the ocean. Presently, a woman dressed in a blue uniform entered the reception area through the security door.

'Good afternoon. I'm Cristin Reid,' she said with a smile and extended her hand towards Fitzjohn. 'I'm told you're making inquiries in regard to Greta Mowbray.'

'Not as such, Ms Reid,' Fitzjohn replied as he shook her hand. 'In actual fact we're here to inquire about those who visit her.'

'Oh I see. Well, Greta only has one visitor, her niece, who comes several times a week.'

'Not her daughter, Stephanie Mowbray?' asked Fitzjohn.

'No. I think I'd be right in saying that I've only seen her daughter on two occasions which were shortly after her mother was admitted to the nursing home and about six months later at Christmas time in 2017. She arrived, seemingly, to have her mother sign some papers. Of course, she could have visited her mother when I wasn't on duty but, to be honest, I rather doubt it.'

'Why is that?' asked Fitzjohn.

'From the odd comments made by Greta from time to time. She may have dementia but there are times she's quite lucid. In those moments, she expresses her disappointment that Stephanie never visits her. Sadly, she blames herself. It must be a heavy burden for her.'

'And the niece who does come to see her?'

'Her name is Elizabeth Tippet. She visits regularly. As a matter of fact, she's here now if you'd like to speak to her.'

'We would,' replied Fitzjohn.

'This is an unexpected development,' said Betts as the two men waited once again.

'All part of the journey,' replied Fitzjohn. 'Like peeling an onion layer by layer. You never know what you'll find.' As he spoke, a woman in her mid-thirties entered the reception area. Wearing a slim fitting grey woollen dress with a long colourful scarf draped around her shoulders and exuding an elegant flare, she walked over to the two officers with a degree of apprehension. Fitzjohn glanced at Betts.

'Hello. I'm Elizabeth Tippet,' said the woman. 'I understand you wish to speak to me about my aunt. I hope there isn't a problem concerning her residency here.'

'Not at all, Ms Tippet,' replied Fitzjohn, gesturing to a nest of chairs set near the window. 'We're merely making inquiries in connection to our investigation and your aunt's name has been raised,' continued Fitzjohn as they sat down. 'We're trying to establish who comes to see your aunt.'

'Oh? Can I ask what sort of investigation you're conducting, Chief Inspector?'

'We're investigating two homicides.'

'*Homicides.*' Elizabeth stared at Fitzjohn. 'I don't see how they could involve my aunt unless... Were they people Aunt Greta knew?'

'I don't believe so,' replied Fitzjohn. 'Our inquiries merely centre on who visited your aunt on Wednesday July 11.'

'I see. Well, that would be me,' replied Elizabeth.

'No one else came to see her?' asked Fitzjohn.

'I rather doubt it. I was here with Aunt Greta for most of

that day and evening because she hadn't been well. I arrived around twelve-thirty in the afternoon and stayed later than usual. Until about eleven that evening, I think. I didn't leave until she'd fallen asleep.'

'So you didn't see her daughter, Stephanie, at all that day?'

'*Stephanie?*' No, not on that day or any other for that matter.'

'We're led to believe she did come to see her mother not long after she was admitted to the facility and again six months later.'

'Evidently she did. I was informed by one of the nurses on duty at the time. They thought I should know because my aunt had become upset. Apparently, Stephanie wanted her to sign an enduring power of attorney. Thankfully, Aunt Greta was lucid on both occasions and refused.' Elizabeth paused. 'I'm not saying that such a document isn't helpful for both parties at a time like this, Chief Inspector, but only if your chosen attorney has your best interests at heart and not their own. Unfortunately, I doubt that is the case where Stephanie is concerned.' Elizabeth hesitated. 'What exactly is this all about, Chief Inspector, because to be honest your questions are unusual?'

'I'm afraid I'm not at liberty to say, Ms Tippet. All I can tell you is that our questions are to confirm information that we've received from persons of interest.'

'I take it Stephanie is one of those persons,' said Elizabeth as she met Fitzjohn's gaze.

'She is,' replied Fitzjohn.

'Momentarily, Elizabeth covered her face with her hands before she continued. 'You'll have to excuse me, Chief Inspector. It's a bit of a sore point with me, I'm afraid. Not that I mind visiting my aunt or paying for her care, she's my mother's sister after all. But as you can imagine it is expensive and a bit of help or even support from Steph wouldn't go amiss, but this is something I didn't expect.'

'Are you saying that you are solely responsible for your aunt's care,' asked Fitzjohn taken aback by this latest revelation.

'Yes. When it became obvious that Aunt Greta needed full-time care, I approached Stephanie but she refused to acknowledge the fact, so I made all the arrangements and have been responsible for the financial side of things ever since.'

'Can you tell us what method the nursing home uses for the payments, Ms Tippet?'

'Of course. It's by direct debit from my bank account each month. It's the only option the nursing home provides.'

Dark clouds gathered over the ocean and a strong wind drove the first drops of rain as Fitzjohn and Betts left the nursing home and sprinted to their car. Slamming the doors as the storm intensified, Fitzjohn settled back in his seat before removing his rain splattered glasses to wipe the lenses. 'We made it just in time,' he said with a chuckle as the car rocked with the force of the wind.

'I think we should wait here until this storm passes,' said Betts as he peered out at the trees and foliage being ravaged by the wind. 'You were right about the onion analogy, sir. Peeling back the layers revealed more than I expected about Stephanie Mowbray. She and her cousin look so alike. It's uncanny.'

'And explains why the description the nursing home staff

gave you the other day led us to believe Mowbray had told us the truth about her whereabouts on July 11.'

'Not to mention the power of attorney she wanted her mother to sign; under duress, by all accounts,' Betts added. 'And I thought she was so caring about her mother's welfare. It just shows how wrong you can be.'

'It's always best to question and not to accept anything at face value,' said Fitzjohn. 'And it's given us the breakthrough we needed to progress with our investigation now we know she doesn't have an alibi for the night of Dolores Madden's murder. And there's also the fact that she isn't financially responsible for payments to the nursing home, so we have to ask why she lied and what happened to the money she has been taking out of her bank account regularly over the past year.'

'It's enough to bring her in for questioning, sir. I'll get that arranged as soon as I get back to the station.'

As Betts spoke, Fitzjohn's mobile phone rang. 'It's internal affairs, no doubt with news of my fate,' he said as he looked at the screen and went to answer it. 'Fitzjohn here. Very well, I'll be there. The tribunal wants to speak to me in their offices at nine o'clock tomorrow morning,' he said as he hung up.

'In that case, it's going to be a long night, sir,' said Betts as he started the car.

Absorbed with thoughts of his meeting with the tribunal the following morning and what the outcome would be, Fitzjohn arrived home, his hand fumbling in his pocket for his front door key. As the door opened, he stepped into the warmth, his nostrils taking in the aroma of food. He smiled to himself at the comforts of home as he placed his briefcase on the hall table. The sight of Meg's suitcase at the foot of the stairs, however, caught his eye and caused him to hesitate, a sense of impending doom taking hold. This can only mean one thing, he thought. Meg is angry.

'Alistair, where on earth have you been?' Taken aback, Fitzjohn swung around to see Meg, her face contorted with rage and he braced himself. 'Since Martin had to work, you said you'd be at Sophie's new apartment when the furniture arrived and help us unpack.'

'That was today?' replied Fitzjohn, crestfallen. 'I do apologise.'

'It's Sophie you should apologise to, not me. I can't believe you forgot, unless...' Meg's eyebrows knitted together. 'You were with Martin weren't you; working on the case despite your suspension.' Fitzjohn did not reply. 'Do you realise you might have put his career on the line?'

'In hindsight, yes, I do. It was selfish of me.'

'Selfish isn't the word. I'm appalled,' said Meg.

'Is that why you're leaving?' asked Fitzjohn, aware that his compulsion to continue his investigation despite his suspension had also caused difficulties for Sophie and undone all that had been gained in his relationship with his sister.

'No, it isn't. I just feel that now Sophie is settled into her new life with Martin and starting out in her career, it's time for me to return home to Melbourne, not to mention the fact that I'm anxious to begin my new gardening project.' Meg broke off and pursed her lips. 'Don't think for one minute it means I'm not still angry with you, Alistair.'

'I don't. You have every right to be angry,' replied Fitzjohn relieved that, at least, his actions had not altered his sister's new-found zest for life. 'I'll give Sophie a call now and apologise.'

'That's the least you can do. You might also consider finding a house-warming gift. It'll help fill your time while you're on suspension.'

'I'll do that too,' said Fitzjohn as he dialled Sophie's number.

When he entered the kitchen some time later, he found Meg at the table setting out an array of brochures, each with a greenhouse depicted on its cover. 'I want to ask your advice on which greenhouse you think would be ideal for my purpose, Alistair.'

'I'd be delighted,' he said as he joined her at the table.

'I know this is a difficult time for you,' said Meg as she watched him scan each brochure. 'Please don't think my returning home means I'm not concerned about your present situation because I am.'

'I know that, Meg.'

'So, you also know I'm always available on the other end of the telephone if you need to talk.'

'I do and that's reassuring,' replied Fitzjohn, unaccustomed to his sister's transformation and hoping it would be permanent.

'Oh.'

'What is it?' asked Fitzjohn.

'It's about Rhonda Butler. How could I have forgotten? There's news. This afternoon, I spoke to her sister, Blossom, and apparently Rhonda's been let off on a one year good behaviour bond.' Fitzjohn looked up from the brochures.

'Blossom's reaction surprised me though. She appeared amused about the whole affair but I'm sure Rhonda isn't. In fact, it set me thinking, Alistair. It might be wise to start making plans to move. After all, your relationship with Mrs Butler will be at a new low. If you stay here you might not be safe in your own home after this debacle.'

'Did Blossom mention what happened to Rhonda's nephew?' asked Fitzjohn.

'Apparently, he received a two year good behaviour bond; I imagine because of his age and the fact that he's never been involved in any sort of criminal activity in the past. He's also been expelled from that posh school he attended.'

With Meg happily absorbed with his greenhouse suggestions, Fitzjohn poured himself a glass of whisky and settled himself into a chair in the conservatory, his thoughts covering the events of the day and coming to rest on his meeting the following morning with internal affairs where he would learn his fate.

CHAPTER 20

*A*ware that his meeting with the internal affairs unit could alter his life completely, Fitzjohn tried to come to terms with that possibility as his taxi weaved through the traffic on its way to the CBD. Straightening his suit coat and adjusting his tie as he entered the building, he took the elevator to the thirteenth floor and emerged straight into the unit's reception area. Deserted but for a woman in attendance behind a desk at the far end of the room, Fitzjohn approached and showed his warrant card.

'I'm DCI Fitzjohn. I'm scheduled to appear before the tribunal at nine o'clock.' he said.

'Ah, yes, Chief Inspector,' she replied with a smile. 'You're to see Chief Superintendents Marshall, Parker, and Fairday. Please take a seat and I'll call you shortly.'

With a growing sense of vulnerability, Fitzjohn settled himself into a chair and waited, a myriad of thoughts crisscrossing his mind, not the least being that this was a watershed moment where his life could alter forever.

'They're ready for you now, Chief Inspector. This way, please.'

Fitzjohn got to his feet and, with a degree of nervous anticipation, followed the young woman along several corridors before being led into a large room, its windows overlooking the city skyline. Three uniformed police officers sat facing the door on the far side of a long table. Remaining seated, they looked up from their paperwork when Fitzjohn appeared in the doorway.

'Chief Inspector Fitzjohn, please come in,' said the officer in the centre. 'I'm CS Marshall and this is CS Parker and CS Fairday. Thank you for coming in at such short notice,' he continued, gesturing to the single chair on the opposite side of the table. Fitzjohn settled himself into his chair with a degree of apprehension.

'Firstly,' said Marshall, 'I should inform you that this isn't a formal tribunal into the incident you have been accused of but merely a discussion, the reason being that after studying the evidence put before us into the matter, we believe you have no case to answer.' Fitzjohn felt a flood of relief and gave an involuntary sigh. 'Our findings are that you found yourself in an unusual situation concerning a neighbour and were in the process of dealing with the occurrence when it was taken out of your hands. We regret that, with your many years of exemplary service as a police officer in the force, this situation occurred and we apologise for the distress it, no doubt, caused you. Consequently, your suspension is hereby lifted and you may resume your duties at Day Street Police Station.'

Little more was said before Fitzjohn left the meeting, pleased he had been vindicated but nonetheless disappointed that his questions had been left unanswered. Had, the tribunal examined Constable Smithers' motivation for his accusation? If so, did their inquiries expose Inspector Grieg's involvement? He supposed the answer to both questions was, yes, but what action would be taken, if any?

Fitzjohn returned to Day Street Police Station to be welcomed with a round of applause and pats on the back. With his spirits lifted by the warmth of this reception and a sense of relief that he could now conduct his investigations openly, he made his way through the station to his office. As the door opened, however, a sense of emptiness took hold as he looked around at the walls and surfaces stripped of all his familiar possessions from his years on the force. All that remained were a couple of chairs, his old swivel seat and the computer screen and keyboard in the centre of his desk. Would that familiar warmth return once his possessions were again in place, he wondered? Stepping inside, he shrugged out of his suit coat, placed it on the back of his chair and was about to take his seat, when a tap on the door sounded.

'Welcome back, Fitzjohn. I've just heard your suspension has been revoked. I'm so pleased.'

'Thank you, ma'am,' Fitzjohn replied, looking into Peta's sparkling blue eyes. 'I won't hide the fact that it's a relief,' he continued as they both sat down.

'It should never have happened and, as your commanding officer, I feel I should have done more.'

'You did warn me about Smithers. I should have taken more notice.'

'Well, he won't be causing you or anyone else here at the

station problems in the future because he's being transferred out of the city to a small town on the south coast.'

'Oh? Is that wise?' asked Fitzjohn. 'After all, sometimes it's best to keep one's adversaries close by.'

'Perhaps but since that course of action has been recommended by internal affairs, I've decided to follow it,' replied Peta. 'I don't want my station to be used as a place where people can vent their vindictiveness. At least this way he'll be out from under Grieg's influence with a chance to make a success of his career in the force.'

'I hope that's the case,' Fitzjohn replied, choosing not to voice his thoughts in regard to Smithers' judgmental personality. 'And what about Grieg's involvement? Any word on that?'

'Since Smithers told all in an effort to save his career, Inspector Grieg's fate is being decided as we speak. And since his banishment to the farthest reaches of the state hasn't curtailed his dirty deeds, I believe the penalty will be severe.' Fitzjohn did not respond, his mind recalling his years of friction with Grieg. 'I'll let you know their ruling as soon as I've heard.' Peta paused as their eye met and an awkward silence ensued. 'Anyway, I'll leave you to settle in,' she said at last, getting to her feet. 'I'm sure you're keen to get on with your investigations.'

'Before you go, ma'am,' said Fitzjohn, 'There's another matter. I'd like to propose that DS Betts be recommended for promotion.'

'As a matter of fact, I've been considering it myself, Fitzjohn. Especially since he took over the investigations with such confidence during your suspension. He deserves it. I'll see what I can do.'

In the incident room, Fitzjohn stood in front of the white-board, familiarising himself once again with the investigations so far. As he surveyed the situation, he heard the door open and turned to see Betts' tall shape.

'Sir. I heard about your reinstatement,' he said with a smile. 'Congratulations.'

'Thank you, Betts, and thank you for supporting me. I owe you a debt of gratitude. Don't think I don't appreciate it.'

'I'm just relieved the situation has been resolved without issue.'

'I can't deny I am too. When I arrived to meet with the tribunal this morning, the last thing I thought was that I'd been standing here now.' Fitzjohn turned back to the white-board. 'I've just been going over everything,' he continued. 'Is there anything I should know?'

'I think you're up to speed, sir.'

'On that account, we'll begin by obtaining search warrants for Stephanie Mowbray's residence and business premises. To be done simultaneously. What we do from there will depend on what we uncover, if anything,' Fitzjohn added.

'Yes, sir.'

Accompanied by three uniformed police officers, Fitzjohn and Betts, arrived at Stephanie Mowbray's home on the north shore in mid-afternoon. 'According to Ms Mowbray's shop assistant, we'll only find her housekeeper at the residence, although Ms Mowbray herself, is due home shortly,'

said Betts as they made their way through the garden to the front door.

'As long as there's someone here to receive us, it's of no concern unless we need to take Ms Mowbray in for questioning,' replied Fitzjohn as he rang the doorbell. Moments went by before the deadlock could be heard being released and the door opened to reveal a woman in her late forties with short, dark hair dressed in a blue uniform. As she appeared, a look of alarm came to her face at the site of the five men.

'Can I help you?' she asked, her eyes darting from Fitzjohn to Betts before they went to the three officers hovering on the edge of the porch.

'We're from the police, madam,' replied Fitzjohn, presenting his warrant card. 'We have a warrant to search these premises.'

'You must have the wrong house.'

'This is the home of Stephanie Mowbray, isn't it?' asked Fitzjohn.

'Yes.'

'In that case, we do have the right address, madam.'

'I can't let you in.' said the woman, her head shaking. 'Not without Ms Mowbray's permission.'

'That being so, it's my duty to inform you that it's an offence to restrict our entrance. I have here an "occupier's notice" issued by the Magistrate's Court that sets out the details in the search warrant.'

The housekeeper swallowed hard as she read the notice before moving back from the doorway in silence. As she did, a car pulled up at the curb and Stephanie Mowbray emerged and strutted through the gate towards them.

'What's going on?' she asked as she reached the front porch.

Fitzjohn turned to face her. 'Ah, good afternoon, Ms Mowbray. We have a warrant to search your premises and your place of business in the Strand Arcade for anything pertaining to our investigation into the death of Dolores Madden.' As he spoke, he presented the occupier's notice once again.

'This is ridiculous.' Stephanie grabbed the notice and ran her eyes over it officiously. 'I object,' she said, shoving it back at Fitzjohn.

'Nevertheless, Ms Mowbray, you're not at liberty to refuse entry to us,' he replied as the officers made their way inside. Ushering Stephanie in, he followed her into the living room. 'You and I will wait in here while the search is undertaken,' he continued.

Stephanie glared at Fitzjohn before she dropped into an armchair to the side of the fireplace while Fitzjohn circled the room, taking in the art deco style of the furnishings and artwork displayed on the walls.

'I can't imagine what you hope to find concerning Dolores Madden. I hardly knew the woman,' said Stephanie at last.

'That may be so, Ms Mowbray, but in conducting our investigation we have to follow every lead until we come to the one that solves our case. It's a process of elimination. Of course, the downside to this process is that some people's sensibilities are hurt and for that I apologise.'

As the minutes ticked by, Stephanie remained seated with her legs crossed and her fingers tapping the arms of her chair. 'How much longer is this going to take?' she blurted out at last as her irritation grew. 'I have a business to run and

I'm due at my shop before closing time.' As she spoke Betts appeared under the archway into the living room. Fitzjohn joined him and they moved into the front hall.

'We've seized a number of items, sir. A kitchen knife that is thought to be the size and type used in Dolores Madden's murder and a T-shirt found in the bottom of a dresser drawer in the master bedroom. It's been washed but there are fine markings sprayed across the front that could be blood.'

'Is that all?' asked Fitzjohn.

'Yes, sir.'

'Very well. Bag it all up and get it to the lab. Hopefully they'll oblige by getting the results back to us quickly.'

'And Ms Mowbray, sir?'

'Since her recent disappearing act, I think we'll proceed on the side of caution and take her in for questioning.'

'That only gives us a six hour window until we have to release her, sir,' said Betts. 'We may not have the results back from the lab in time.'

'True, but we are allowed one extension so, if time grows short, we'll apply for a detention warrant.'

CHAPTER 21

$\mathcal{A}$s the hours ticked by and the office grew dark with the last vintages of light dipping beneath the city skyline, Fitzjohn paced the floor of his office and waited for news from the lab. As he did so a continual stream of facts concerning Stephanie Mowbray's involvement in Dolores Madden's murder ran through his mind, along with the lack of evidence as to her involvement in Howard Greenwood's death. Was his theory that the two murders were connected wrong? Interrupted by a knock on the door, he turned to see Betts.

'The results are back, sir.'

'And?'

'They're positive. Microscopic traces of Dolores Madden's blood have been found on the knife and on the T-shirt.'

'Excellent,' said Fitzjohn.

'How do you plan to handle the interview, sir? Are you going to concentrate purely on Madden's death? The reason

I ask is that we have very little that connects Stephanie Mowbray to Greenwood's murder.'

'I've been asking myself the same question, Betts. We'll start with Madden and at some point, touch on Greenwood's death and see what reaction we get.'

Stephanie Mowbray sat motionless at the table in the windowless interview room. When the door opened and the two officers walked in, she shot Fitzjohn a damning look. 'How dare you keep me waiting here. I told you, I have a business to run. My time means money.'

'I see you haven't chosen to engage council,' said Fitzjohn, ignoring Mowbray's comments as he sat down and placed two sealed plastic bags containing the knife and the T-shirt on the table in front of him.

'Mowbray looked at the bags. 'Why should I need a lawyer when I haven't done anything wrong?' she replied with an air of false self-assurance.

'It's entirely up to you, Ms Mowbray, but if you should change your mind at any time during the course of the interview process, please let us know and council will be provided,' said Fitzjohn. 'I should also inform you that you are not obliged to answer any questions posed to you.'

'You're not recording this, are you?', barked Mowbray, her attention taken by Betts as he prepared the recording device.

'It's routine, Ms Mowbray,' replied Fitzjohn.

After introductions and the time were recorded, Fitzjohn adjusted his chair and began the interview. 'Ms Mowbray, I'd like to start by asking what your movements were between the hours of four p.m. and midnight on Wednesday, July 11, 2018?'

'You know where I was. I've already told you.'

'Even so, your whereabouts on that day need to be recorded,' replied Fitzjohn.

'*All right, if I must.* I was at the Seaview Nursing Home visiting my mother,' said Mowbray into the machine.

'Are you quite sure about that?' asked Fitzjohn. 'The reason I ask is because we're led to believe you weren't present at the nursing home on that day, nor that evening. In fact, we understand you have only attended the facility on two occasions in the past eighteen months namely, not long after your mother was admitted and the second occasion during the Christmas period of 2017.'

'I don't know who told you that but whoever it is, is lying,' replied Mowbray, raising her voice. 'Do you think I'd pay out all that money for my mother's care without making sure the nursing home is looking after her properly?'

'But you don't pay out any money for her care, do you Ms Mowbray?' replied Fitzjohn, sitting forward in his chair. 'Your cousin, Elizabeth Tippett, has been financially responsible for your mother's care since she entered the nursing home. She's also the person who visits your mother several times a week and has done so since she entered the facility.'

Mowbray avoided Fitzjohn's gaze and looked away to some point on the opposite wall behind the two officers. Fitzjohn pushed the plastic bags into the centre of the table and waited for Mowbray's attention. 'As you're aware, we seized these items, a kitchen knife and a T-shirt, from your residence during our search of the property and they have since been analysed by forensic services,' he continued. 'I should inform you that the knife has been identified as the weapon used in

Dolores Madden's murder. This assumption is supported by the fact that traces of her blood were found on the knife. Evidence of Ms Madden's blood was also found on the T-shirt.'

'That's impossible,' Mowbray snapped.

'Blood doesn't lie, Ms Mowbray, and detergent doesn't remove such evidence.'

'So, what are you saying? That I murdered Dolores.'

'We know you did,' Fitzjohn replied, his hand resting on the plastic bag that held the knife. 'And since there are similarities with Howard Greenwood's death, we...'

'Wait a minute. You're not accusing me of his murder too, are you?'

'As I said, there are similarities in that long-stemmed red roses were found thrown over each body. Such an act has to be planned and since the evidence against you concerning Dolores Madden's murder is unmistakable, it stands to reason that you are also responsible for Howard Greenwood's death.'

'But the roses were already there...' Mowbray stiffened as she realised her admission. 'You bastard.' Mowbray grabbed the glass of water on the table in front of her and gulped it down before she slumped back in her chair.

'So you admit to the murder of Dolores Madden.'

Mowbray glared at Fitzjohn. 'All right, yes, but it doesn't mean I killed Howard.'

'Since all the evidence points to the fact you did, you'll have to convince us otherwise,' said Fitzjohn.

'What other evidence do you have other than the damn roses?' barked Mowbray.

'For a start, the fact that Howard Greenwood planned to expose you as his wife's killer.'

'But that's ridiculous. You've got it all wrong. I didn't kill Howard or Marsha. I had no reason to.'

'I think you did,' said Fitzjohn. 'I believe you killed Dolores because she was blackmailing you over Marsha Greenwood's death. After all, the money you claimed you paid out in nursing home fees had to go somewhere.' Mowbray did not respond. 'Well?'

'Okay. Okay. She was blackmailing me but not for the reason you think.' Mowbray hesitated. 'You've got to understand. I'm a dress designer. My clothes are sold around the world.'

'And?'

'And Dolores threatened to expose me.'

'For doing what?' asked Fitzjohn.

'She found out - I don't know how – that in the recent past, I'd stolen a prominent couturier's designs. She threatened to expose me if I didn't pay her so I agreed because it would have ruined my name. I'd never have worked again. Don't you see?' Mowbray's eyes darted between the two officers. 'It's true. I swear. It had nothing to do with Marsha's death.'

'It doesn't change the fact that we believe both murders at the Adelphi Theatre were perpetrated by the same person which is you, Ms Mowbray. Not to mention the fact that the reason you killed Howard Greenway was because he planned to expose you as the person who pushed his wife down the stairs.'

'But I didn't push her. Madelaine did,' screamed Mowbray, tears brimming her eyelids.

As Stephanie Mowbray sobbed, Fitzjohn waited for a moment before he said, 'Are you saying that Madelaine Wells pushed Marsha Greenwood down the stairs at the 2017 Christmas party?'

'Yes.'

'How do you know this?'

'Because… I saw her do it. I'd gone upstairs to the powder room. When I came out, Marsha and Dolores were arguing on the landing.'

'Was Ms Wells aware you were there?'

'No, of course not.'

'Did you hear what their argument was about?'

'The play, what else? Madelaine wanted Marsha's role. And it was obvious she had her eye on Howard as well.'

'Why didn't you come forward at the coroner's inquest?'

'Because I didn't want to get involved, particularly with Dolores blackmailing me. The media attention would have been horrendous.'

Fitzjohn sat back in his chair in an effort to ponder this latest revelation before he said, 'Ms Mowbray, I'd like to go back for a moment to Wednesday, July 11, the night Dolores was murdered. Can you tell me what time you entered the theatre?'

'It was around 5 p.m.'

'How did you know Dolores would be there? After all, that was the day the theatre closed.'

'I know, but she told me that's where I had to meet her on that day.'

'Did you always pay her in cash?'

'Always,' replied Mowbray.

'I see. And when you arrived, did you see anyone else on the premises?'

'No. There was no one else there.'

'What time did you leave?' asked Fitzjohn.

'It was just after five-thirty. I think.'

'What do you think, sir?' asked Betts as the two officers left the interview room.

'She says she left the Adelphi at about 5:30 pm. I seem to remember Constance Parsons said she didn't arrive until six o'clock that evening which means...'

'Even though she has admitted to killing Dolores Madden, she couldn't have attacked Ms Parsons,' put in Betts.

'Exactly. Of course, there's every possibility she might be lying since it will connect her to Howard Greenwood's murder. I don't want her charged until we know for sure and to do that we need to speak to Madelaine Wells again.'

'We're running short on the amount of time we have left to hold Mowbray, sir,' said Betts, looking at his watch. 'I'll apply for a detention warrant and I'll have Ms Wells brought in for questioning.'

'Also apply for a search warrant for her residence and dressing room at the State Theatre,' said Fitzjohn.

'Yes, sir.'

CHAPTER 22

*I*n the incident room, Fitzjohn made adjustments to the whiteboard by adding the recent evidence gathered from Stephanie Mowbray as Dolores Madden's killer. Was she also guilty of Howard Greenwood's, he mused and, was she the person who attacked Constance Parsons? That theory fell easily into place, but was it the right one? As he looked up at the clock on the wall, the door at the rear of the room opened.

'Ah, Betts, how did you get on?'

'You were right to have searches conducted, sir. Nothing untoward was found at Wells' residence but in her dressing room at the State Theatre we found written notes stashed in her handbag. I suspect they concern the last chapter of Greenwood's memoir and possibly taken during the break-in at his home. I've sent them to the lab for analysis but I do have a copy for you here.' Betts passed Fitzjohn the folder he held in his hand.

'Good work,' said Fitzjohn opening the folder. 'It's more than I'd hoped for,' he continued as he ran his eyes over the pages. 'He clearly states here that Madelaine Wells deliberately pushed his wife, Marsha Greenwood, down the stairs and he plans to see her pay for her crime.' Fitzjohn looked up. 'Did Wells offer an explanation as to how the notes came to be in her possession?'

'No, sir. She was fairly taken aback when we arrived and was less than cooperative.'

'Any evidence concerning the roses?' asked Fitzjohn, placing the notes back into the folder before handing it to Betts.

'No, sir, but there is one interesting factor that's turned up. Remember the photograph that remained intact on Howard Greenwood's study wall?'

'Ah, yes. Mrs Evans identified it as a photograph of Howard Greenwood and his wife on stage on the play's opening night. I seem to remember the back of the frame had been tampered with.'

'That's right,' said Betts. 'Tampered with so that the photograph could be replaced. The lab has identified the two people on stage as Howard Greenwood and Madelaine Wells. I checked with theatre management who confirmed the photograph was taken on Wells' first performance in the female lead.'

'Bizarre behaviour, don't you think?' said Fitzjohn. 'It makes me wonder what exactly we're dealing with here.'

Fitzjohn and Betts entered the interview room to find Madelaine Wells applying lipstick by way of the room's two way mirror while her assigned lawyer, a young man impeccably dressed in a dark blue suit sat at the table. She looked around when the two officers appeared in the doorway but, unmoved by their presence, she gave her lips a further coat.

'Good evening, Ms Wells. Please take a seat and we'll commence the interview,' said Fitzjohn as he pulled out a chair.

With an air of complacency, Madelaine thrust the lipstick into its tube, tossed it into her handbag and, throwing back her head, glided across the floor. Glowering at the three men, she sat down, her tight fitting turquoise dress riding up along her shapely legs. Aware of her attempt at diversion, Fitzjohn sat down and cleared his throat. Madelaine's lawyer, transfixed by the scene, flinched, adjusted his chair and rearranged his papers.

As the interview got underway, Fitzjohn placed a plastic sleeve, containing the presumed notes on the last chapter of Greenwood's memoir, on the table. 'Ms Wells, can you tell us how you came to have these papers in your possession?'

'Howard left them in my dressing room one night at the Adelphi Theatre after a performance,' replied Madelaine indignantly. 'When the theatre closed down they must have been packed up with the rest of my belongings. I didn't even know they were in my dressing room until your sergeant found them.'

'I think that's highly unlikely since they were found in your handbag,' said Fitzjohn. 'Now, why don't you tell us the truth since lying will only serve to make things more difficult for you. I say that because we believe these papers were stolen from Howard Greenwood's home in the early hours on Saturday, July 8, the day after his death.'

'I wouldn't know anything about that since I was at home that morning recovering from my migraine the previous night,' said Madelaine, shifting in her chair.

'Ah, yes, how could I forget,' said Fitzjohn. 'You explained it all to us, didn't you, during our first discussion. You said you arrived home at around eleven p.m.'

'That's right.'

'And yet, we have a witness who saw you in the laneway outside the Adelphi at twelve-thirty that night.'

Madelaine glared at Fitzjohn. 'Whoever said that is mistaken. You know I went home. I showed you the Uber fare on my iPhone.'

'So you did. However, there was nothing to stop you going back to the theatre, Ms Wells,' said Fitzjohn.

'To do what?' Madelaine hesitated. 'Wait a minute. You're not suggesting I killed Howard are you?'

'These notes imply he was planning on publishing his memoir that accuses you of killing his wife.' Fitzjohn placed his hand on the plastic sleeve containing the notes. 'These have been found in your possession. We also have a witness who saw you at the crime scene just before Howard Green-wood was murdered, so yes, Ms Wells, we are suggesting you killed him.'

'It's not enough to charge me with their murders.'

'I think you'll find it is,' replied Fitzjohn, 'because one of your victim's didn't die, a fact I'm sure you're well aware of since you've attempted to terrorise her with two bouquets of long-stemmed red roses.' Madelaine did not reply. 'Not only that,' continued Fitzjohn, 'it so happens she has a clear memory of your assault on her and has identified you. Of course, the roses make our cases even stronger since they're also involved in two of the three murders.'

Madelaine glared at Fitzjohn, 'You can't accuse me of murdering three people.'

'I think you'll find we can,' said Fitzjohn. 'Howard Greenwood, his wife Marsha, and Dolores Madden.'

'But I didn't kill Dolores. And Marsha fell.'

'We have a witness who says you pushed her. If you have another scenario, now is the time to tell us.' Madelaine's eyes darted between the two officers. 'Well?' asked Fitzjohn, sensing Madelaine's rising confusion as she attempted to clarify her answers.

'All right, we did argue at the top of the stairs that night, but it was when Marsha gave me a shove and I pushed her arm away that she became unbalanced and fell. It was an accident, but Howard wouldn't believe me.'

'He spoke to you about it?' asked Fitzjohn with a grimace.

'Yes, while we were on stage. Subtle remarks in my ear saying he would expose me for all the world to see as his wife's killer through that damn memoir he was writing. On the last night of the play he said it wouldn't be long because he was putting the finishing touches to the final chapter. I panicked. I had to stop him publishing it.'

'So, you returned to the theatre?' Fitzjohn waited for Madelaine to answer.

'Yes,' she replied at last with an air of despondency. 'I knew he'd stay on for a while after everyone had left the party because he was sentimental about the theatre's closure.' Madelaine smiled. 'The look on his face when I opened the door. It was priceless. He didn't know what to expect. He started ranting. Told me to get out. That's when I snapped. I grabbed the first thing I could get my hands on which was a rolled up newspaper and lashed out at him. I had to shut him up.'

'And the roses?'

'They were in a vase on the dresser. I thought they added an amusing touch.'

'And they became your signature because you used them in Dolores Madden's killing as well, didn't you?' prompted Fitzjohn.

'I've already told you, I didn't kill Dolores. She was already dead when I got to the theatre.' Madelaine chuckled. 'Such a spectacle couldn't have happened at a better time. I thought the ghost writer would die right there on the spot before I got a chance to finish her off myself. And I would have in the end; given a little more time.'

'If you didn't kill Dolores, how do you explain the roses thrown over her body?' asked Fitzjohn.

'Dolores always collected the flowers thrown after a performance and put them in water. On the last night they just happened to be long-stemmed red roses. I suppose her killer found them and mimicked me. It annoyed me because, as you said, long-stemmed red roses are my signature, no one else's.'

'So it appears,' replied Fitzjohn as he began to question Madelaine's psychological state of mind. 'Tell me, Ms Wells, with the theatre now closed down, where did you get your supply for those you sent to the ghost writer?'

'You mean you don't know? I would have thought a clever detective like you would have worked that out. Maybe it was just too easy because I used the Sydney markets. There are always flowers for sale.'

'Read Ms Wells her rights, Detective Sergeant Betts,' said Fitzjohn as he got to his feet and left the room.

~

In the wee hours, Peta Ashby's office door stood ajar exposing its dark interior as Fitzjohn walked through the station to the canteen. Deserted and silent but for the hum of the coffee machine, he took a cup from the tray at the side and filled it with the strong aromatic liquid before settling himself at one of the tables. Cradling the cup in his grasp, he took a sip and sighed, the culmination of the day's events lending to a sense of satisfaction. When the door opened, he looked up to see Betts.

'Just to let you know, sir, Madelaine Wells and Stephanie Mowbray are being processed,' he said as he poured himself a cup of coffee and joined Fitzjohn at the table. 'I just need to complete the paperwork.'

'Excellent. And I'll get started on my reports to the chief superintendent so I can give them to her in the morning.' Fitzjohn finished his coffee and set his cup down. 'I'll also speak to Constance Parsons to put her mind at rest with the news the killers are behind bars. Hopefully, despite the trauma she's been through, she can get her life back to normal.' Fitzjohn shook his head. 'They haven't been easy cases to solve and I have to admit, there were times I had my doubts we'd be successful.'

'They've were among the most baffling cases we've had, sir, but we got there in the end and with a twist I didn't expect. I'd all but come to the conclusion that Mowbray was the killer.'

'To be honest, I was leaning that way myself until the missing link, being Marsha Greenwood's death, surfaced,' said Fitzjohn. 'And we still might not have been successful if Wells hadn't mentally collapsed. I'm sure there's a serious underlying problem there, Betts.'

'I have her scheduled for a mental health assessment, sir.'

'Good, because I have a feeling Howard Greenwood's continued intimidation sent her over the edge. The coroner's finding of death by misadventure must have been an affront to his senses since he knew the truth.'

'A tragic outcome for both he and his wife,' said Betts, getting to his feet. 'I'd better get started on that paperwork.'

'Before you go,' said Fitzjohn joining Betts as he left the canteen. 'I want to apologise for putting your career at risk during my suspension. It was selfish and reckless of me.'

'I could have refused, sir.'

'That's beside the point. I should never have asked.' Fitzjohn watched Betts walk ahead, his thoughts a mixture of satisfaction in having solved the case yet tinged with a rising feeling of disquiet.

With his reports on the Greenwood and Madden homicides along with a further report for the assault on Constance Parsons complete, Fitzjohn shrugged into his suit coat and, with a glance across the room, switched off the office light and left the station. He emerged into the cold night air and climbing into the waiting taxi sat back with a sigh, the events of the day flooding over him.

With Meg now back home in Melbourne, his cottage emitted no welcoming light through the stained-glass front door as he made his way along the garden path to the porch and turned the key in the lock. As he stepped inside, the clock on the mantelpiece in the living room chimed twice, filling the silence. He hesitated for a moment and looked in the direction of the kitchen doorway at the end of the hall almost expecting his sister to appear with her cheery greeting – well, on most occasions, he thought with a chuckle. Even so, the emptiness left by her departure was evident. Weary, he placed his briefcase on the hall table at the same time catching his image in the mirror above. Puzzled, he paused and became acutely aware of a rising sense of unrest. Surely it can't be Meg's absence, he thought. It must be with the investigation coming to an end. It tends to be somewhat of an anti-climax. With a sigh, he turned off the hall light and climbed the stairs.

CHAPTER 23

*D*espite his exhaustion, Fitzjohn tossed and turned throughout the night only to wake in the early hours of the morning with his sense of disquiet still evident. Determined to push it to the back of his mind, he pulled on his old gardening clothes and made his way outside, pausing on the back porch to take in the freshness of the air and listen to the birds gathered in the trees above.

'Good morning, Mr Fitzjohn.'

Startled, Fitzjohn turned to see Blossom on the other side of the hedge. Dressed in a colourful floral gown, her hair swept up and held with a matching scarf, she flicked the ash from her cigarette before putting it to her lips.

'Good morning, Mrs Carey,' he said as he stepped off the porch. 'How's your sister after her ordeal?' he asked with genuine concern.

Blossom exhaled a stream of smoke into the damp air. 'She's planning her revenge on you, I'd say,' replied Blossom with a chuckle.

'I regret the matter went as far as it did. I really do,' said Fitzjohn. 'I'll drop in to see her this morning.'

'If you value your life I don't think you should do that, Mr Fitzjohn,' replied Blossom. 'Especially since I won't be here to calm her down when she sets eyes on you. You see, I'm leaving for home very shortly.'

'Well, in that event, perhaps I should leave it for a few days,' replied Fitzjohn. 'Have a good journey and I'll no doubt see you the next time you come to visit.'

'You will, although I doubt it'll top this stay with Rhonda being arrested.'

'Mmm. I realise it must have caused you a great deal of anxiety.'

'Quite the opposite,' replied Blossom. 'I can't thank you enough. I've enjoyed every minute. It's the best thing that's ever happened to my sister.' Blossom paused. 'I suppose you think that sounds unkind, Mr Fitzjohn. But, you see, I've spent my whole life being the black sheep of my family, with both Rhonda and my brother, Edwin, never putting a foot wrong. I can't help but feel pleased that they've both fallen from their high perches even if Edwin's plunge was as a result of his son's illegal activities.' With a wide smile, Blossom waved and disappeared into the house.

Fitzjohn raised his hand in a wave as Blossom vanished from view, mystified that she could be related to Rhonda. Perhaps she's adopted and doesn't know it, he thought as he carried on along the garden path to the greenhouse. Opening the door, he switched on the CD player and the sound of Chopin's Etude in E Flat filled the air. Turning, he surveyed the rows of orchids with their diverse colours and shapes standing erect in the morning stillness aware that his feeling of unease had surfaced once again. Maybe it's not the completion of the investigation that's making me feel this way, he thought as he began to tend each plant. It could be my suspension. Perhaps it affected me more than I realised at the time. It has to be that because it can't be the fact that Meg has gone home to Melbourne. After all, I'm happy she's embracing a new interest in life. Time is what I need. Time to get back into my routine.

Ignoring his unease and in an effort to have his reports on the investigations in front of the chief superintendent when she arrived at the station that morning, Fitzjohn left for work early. On arrival, he entered the building carrying his box of belongings under his arm, his thoughts filled with re-establishing himself in his office. When he opened the door, however, he stopped on its threshold, his grip on the box tightening. 'Who am I fooling but myself?' he muttered at last. Placing the box on his desk, he removed the reports from his briefcase and left the room to make his way along the corridor to Peta Ashby's office where he found her already at work.

'I had hoped to have these on your desk for your arrival,' he said as he walked into the room and handed her the reports.

'Nevertheless, they're timely since I've just finished reading through DS Betts' notes on the cases and I can see how complicated the investigations were, Fitzjohn.' Peta gestured to the chair in front of her desk. 'You're both to be commended.'

'Thank you. They have been baffling cases and I have to admit there were times I had misgivings as to whether we'd be successful,' replied Fitzjohn as his sat down. 'They unravelled in the end, however.'

'They did. And I have some pleasing news as well,' she said. 'Firstly, following your recommendation, DS Betts has been promoted to Detective Senior Sergeant. He was notified early this morning.'

'No one deserves it more,' said Fitzjohn. 'He's a credit to the force.'

'I agree.'

'And the second piece of news?' asked Fitzjohn.

'It concerns Inspector Grieg's fate. Apparently, he was given a choice of resigning from the force or being dismissed. Not surprisingly, he chose the former.'

'He's not a young man. It won't be easy for him,' said Fitzjohn.

'He brought it upon himself, Fitzjohn, and evidently he's fallen on his feet.'

'Oh?'

'Yes. He's now working for the city council as a parking inspector. I think handing out parking fines will suit him down to the ground, don't you?'

'I feel that handing out parking fines to unsuspecting citizens is far from easy, but I doubt Grieg will find it difficult,' replied Fitzjohn before an uneasy silence filled the room.

'Is everything all right, Alistair?' asked Peta, her face full of concern. 'I thought you'd be pleased to see Grieg get his comeuppance.'

'I am, believe me!'

'Is it your suspension? Are you finding it difficult to settle back in again? I can only imagine how traumatic it must have been for you.'

'You're very perceptive,' replied Fitzjohn. 'I've been asking myself the same question and I did think it must be my suspension. That is until I walked into my office a few minutes ago and realised it wasn't that at all.'

'Then what is it?'

'It's time for me to leave the force, Peta.'

'*What!*' Peta stared in disbelief at Fitzjohn.

'I came in here to tender my resignation.'

'But... I don't know what to say,' said Peta, aghast. 'Are you sure you want to do this? Perhaps you should take some time to think it over first because this isn't just your career we're talking about, Alistair, it's your whole life. You are Day Street Police Station.'

'Thank you for the endorsement,' replied Fitzjohn with a chuckle. 'And you're right that the station has been the centre of my life for a very long time and I've been happy here but, I know now that it's time for me to leave.'

Peta stared at Fitzjohn for a long moment. 'You really have made up your mind, haven't you? I can see it in your eyes.'

'Yes, I have,' replied Fitzjohn as a sense of relief flooded through his body. 'I have indeed.'

'Well, it saddens me to see you go, it really does,' said Peta, her eyes glistening. 'What are your plans for the future?'

'To be honest, I have no idea.'

Fitzjohn walked back to his office, the impact of his decision slowly sinking in. At the same time, however, he knew he had done the right thing in facing the fact that remaining at the station was not possible considering his attraction to Peta Ashby. After all, rumours had already started. But if I'm being honest, it isn't the only issue that's driving me, he thought as he opened the door and walked inside. It's much more than that. Opening the cardboard box on his desk, he reached for the frame that held Edith's smiling image. Since you've been gone, I've marked time, he said to himself. I've continued on in the same pattern, holding on to all we held dear, but I know now that the time has come to let you go, Edith. I have to begin again. With a slight hesitation, he blinked back a tear, placed the frame into the box and closed its lid.

'I thought you'd have everything unpacked and in place by now.'

Fitzjohn turned to see Betts in the doorway. 'That was the plan when I arrived this morning,' he said.

'Have you decided to take leave instead?' asked Betts as they sat down.' It's probably the perfect time since we've just finished our investigations.'

'No, not exactly,' replied Fitzjohn. 'I've decided to leave the police force. I've tendered my resignation.' Speechless, Betts stared at his boss. 'I can't explain,' Fitzjohn continued. 'I just know it's what I need to do,'

'Are you sure, sir? I mean...'

'I am, Betts. I think it's just taken me a while to realise it. But that aside, I hear there are congratulations to be given. Your promotion came through.'

'It has. I did hope for a promotion after sitting my promotional exams but I didn't expect it to happen so soon.'

'It's well deserved, Betts. You're an invaluable member of the force. You'll go far.'

CHAPTER 24

*I*n truth, it took Fitzjohn a number of months to acclimatise himself to his new situation, filling his days with his passion for gardening, spending endless hours at the library where he immersed himself in books he previously never had time to seek out, and involving himself fully in the activities of the North Shore Orchid Society. Nevertheless, there were instances when misgivings crept into his thoughts as to whether he had made the right decision, particularly since having resigned from the force his routine had remained the same. Often his thoughts went to Peta Ashby, and he asked himself whether he should call her but each time, he abandoned the idea and remained frustrated with indecision.

It was during one of these instances of indecisiveness that his telephone rang. 'Fitzjohn,' he answered, puzzled by the unknown number on the screen.

'Alistair, it's David Roberts from North Shore Area Command.'

'David, how are you? I don't think we've spoken since the investigation at Lane's End. That was some time ago.'

'It's been a while, hasn't it?,' said David. 'I heard via the grapevine you've left the force. What are you doing now?'

'I'm still deciding.'

'On that account, you might be interested in what I'm calling about. I need a consultant for a homicide case. No footwork involved, just your intellect. Of course, I realise you might not wish to get back into the same kind of work, but give it some thought and let me know.'

And so it was that Fitzjohn's path in life took an unexpected turn and with it a renewed sense of enthusiasm since it led to further consultancies. Now fully settled into his new routine, he made his way into North Sydney Police Station and towards the incident room where the management meeting was about to commence.

'Alistair?'

At the sound of the familiar voice, Fitzjohn turned to see Peta Ashby. 'Ah, this is an unexpected pleasure,' he said, at once captivated by her sparkling blue eyes and warm smile. 'How are you?'

'I'm well. So, is the rumour I heard that you've taken up consultancy work true? Or are you here to make a citizen's complaint?' she added with a chuckle.

'No, the rumour's true. I have the benefits of investigating a case without the stress. Are you arriving or departing?' he asked.

'I'm just on my way back to Day Street otherwise I'd love to stay and catch up.'

'And I'm due in a meeting so… Can I give you a call?' said Fitzjohn unwilling to give away this unexpected opportunity. 'We can arrange something, perhaps.'

'I'd like that. It'll give us the chance to continue our unfinished conversation.' Fitzjohn gave a questioning look. 'Don't you remember? That day at the Charlotte Café. You were about to tell me something when my telephone rang. Something to do with why we were the subject of rumour and a wager.'

'Ah! So I was. I'll tell you over dinner tonight.'

THE END

Cast of Characters

Detective Chief Inspector Alistair Fitzjohn
Detective Sergeant Martin Betts
Chief Superintendent Peta Ashby
Charles Conroy- *Forensic Pathologist*
Detective Senior Constable Williams
Inspector Grieg
Constable Smithers
Meg-*Fitzjohn's sister*
Sophie-*Fitzjohn's niece*
Rhonda Butler-*Fitzjohn's neighbour*
Blossom – *Rhonda's sister*
Edwin – *Rhonda's brother*
Constance Parsons – *Ghost writer*
Harriet Flynn – *Constance's friend*
Howard Greenwood - *Actor*
Leo Greenwood – *Howard's brother*
Lyn Evans – *Howard's housekeeper*
Simon Roach - *Playwright*
Madelaine Wells - *Actress*
Stephanie Mowbray – *Dress designer*
Greta Mowbray – *Stephanie's mother*
Elizabeth Tippett – *Stephanie's cousin*

ABOUT THE AUTHOR

Jill is best known for her Fitzjohn mysteries including The Celtic Dagger, Murder At The Rocks, Once Upon A Lie, Lane's End, Deadly Investment, Poisoned Palette, The Fourth String and Rose Scented Murder. She has also authored two non-fiction books entitled Self Publishing-Pocket Guide and Writing-Painting A Picture With Words.

Born in Yorkshire, UK, Jill now lives in Australia with her musician husband and bossy cat, Fergus. Her favourite pastimes when not writing are painting and photography.

If you would like to get an automatic email when Jill's next book is released, sign up on her blog at https://www.theperfectplot.blogspot.com. Your email address will never be shared and you can unsubscribed at any time.

CPSIA information can be obtained
at www.ICGtesting.com
Printed in the USA
BVHW091334150419
545531BV00021B/620/P

9 780992 584078